WITHDRAWN

WITHDRAWN

WITHDRAWN

EMPTY SMILES

ALSO BY KATHERINE ARDEN

Small Spaces

Dead Voices

Dark Waters

The Bear and the Nightingale

The Girl in the Tower

The Winter of the Witch

EMPTY SMILES

KATHERINE ARDEN

putnam

G. P. PUTNAM'S SONS

G. P. PUTNAM'S SONS
An imprint of Penguin Random House LLC, New York

First published in the United States of America by G. P. Putnam's Sons,
an imprint of Penguin Random House LLC, 2022

G. P. Putnam's Sons is a registered trademark of Penguin Random House LLC.

Visit us online at penguinrandomhouse.com

Library of Congress Cataloging-in-Publication Data
Names: Arden, Katherine, author.
Title: Empty smiles / Katherine Arden.
Description: New York: G. P. Putnam's Sons, 2022. | Series: Small spaces quartet; book 4 |
Summary: "When the carnival arrives in town, Coco, Brian, and Phil must work together
to save Ollie from the smiling man"—Provided by publisher.
Identifiers: LCCN 2022011400 (print) | LCCN 2022011401 (ebook) |
ISBN 9780593109182 (hardcover) | ISBN 9780593109199 (ebook)
Subjects: CYAC: Best friends—Fiction. | Friendship—Fiction. | Carnivals—Fiction. |
Survival—Fiction. | Horror stories. | LCGFT: Horror stories.
Classification: LCC PZ7.1.A737 Em 2022 (print) | LCC PZ7.1.A737 (ebook) | DDC [Fic]—dc23
LC record available at https://lccn.loc.gov/2022011400
LC ebook record available at https://lccn.loc.gov/2022011401

Printed in the United States of America

ISBN 9780593109182
1st Printing

LSCH

Design by Eileen Savage
Text set in Dante MT Pro

To Lilja Bruhn Adler
On your birthday
April 20, 2022
These books were always for you

EMPTY SMILES

Prologue

HIS FRIENDS SAID the carnival that year was special, but Tim Jenkins didn't believe it. The carnival came every year. It was an August tradition. Why would this one be special?

"I think it is," his sister Ruth insisted on the ride out to the fairgrounds. A hot August afternoon was turning into a sultry evening. The cornfields lay densely green on either side of the road. "Riley Temperance said it was. Said it's all different from last year. Different carnies. Different games. Just—different!"

"Sure," Tim admitted. He was two years older. "Maybe it's a little different. But that doesn't mean it's special. Carnivals are boring. I want to watch the demolition derby. Cousin Maynard's in it, you know—he's been working on his car forever." Their car bumped up and down on the dirt road. Hot wind blew dust into Tim's face.

Ruth was craning out her window for a sight of the fairgrounds. Tim didn't think she'd heard him. She said, "Imagine if the carnival was magic. Imagine riding the lion on the merry-go-round and it just comes to life, and it's your friend and you can ride it anywhere." Her voice was dreamy. She pushed her head farther out the window, blinking against the dust.

Tim was unconvinced. "Whatever. Demolition derbies are way more exciting. Besides, imagine if your carousel lion wanted to eat you. You wouldn't be so happy then, would you? Nom nom." Tim crooked his fingers at his sister and clacked his teeth. Ruth shrieked and whacked him in the shoulder.

From the front seat, their mom said, "Hey! Hey, cool it or . . ." She trailed off.

Ruth and Tim stopped fighting. Suddenly, there wasn't any sound in the car except the bleat of fairground music and Vermont Public Radio droning on: "Drought continues to blanket the state, with no sign of precipitation in the extended forecast . . ."

"Wow," Ruth said. She wasn't talking about the extended forecast.

Ordinarily, Tim and his sister didn't agree on anything. But he said wow too. They were all staring out the windows.

The mountains were a blur on the horizon, where the heat haze smeared their outline into the sky. The dusty cornfields rippled, and in the middle of them, in the same spot as last year, was the carnival. But it was, as Riley Temperance had said, completely different.

"I've never seen anything like it," Tim's dad said.

"It's amazing," Tim's mom said.

Ruth didn't say anything else, but her mouth had fallen open.

The Ferris wheel arced over the midway like a moving rainbow. The funhouse was as tall as a castle, with turrets and strange windows. Flags flew from all its highest points. It was covered in mirrors and glittered like an old-timey disco ball.

"Let's go!" Ruth yelled, bouncing in her seat.

"Tim? Stick with your sister, okay?" their mom said. "And don't eat too much sugar."

"'Kay," Tim said, not looking away from the window. The carnival filled his eyes with color and movement. Music and delicious smells drifted out into the hot August evening. Tim wasn't even sure that he wanted to watch the demolition derby anymore. He'd never seen anything as beautiful as that carnival.

His dad said, "We'll meet up at eight. You know the spot—right by the gate. Here's some money. Have fun!"

Tim and Ruth hopped out of the car and ran together through the carnival gates. "Ooh, look at the carnies!" cried Ruth. "That one waved at me!"

Tim didn't answer; he was turning in a delighted circle. The concession stand popped mountains of golden popcorn. The cotton candy machine whirled, spitting out pink clouds of sugar. One of the carnies was tossing handfuls of wrapped chocolates, and kids were catching them and eating them.

Right in the midway, an animatronic clown soared over the fairgrounds. It looked as tall as the Ferris wheel. It was holding a clock in its outstretched hands. Its mouth opened, and its voice boomed across the fairgrounds. Six o'clock, called the clown. HA HA HA.

Tim and Ruth both laughed. It was so silly.

"Looks like we have two hours," Tim said.

Ruth jumped up and down. "Let's play some games! How much did Dad give you?"

Tim looked. "Forty bucks." The carnival smelled so good. Sweet and salty. It was making him hungry. He started toward the concession stand. "But I want popcorn first. And lemonade."

"And funnel cake?"

"Mom said not too much sugar—" He saw Ruth's pleading face. "All right."

They got their snacks. Their faces were covered with sugar and grease. They took long drinks of sour, freezing lemonade. Then they started playing. The games were wicked and fast and fun. Prizes hung from each game-booth ceiling. Most carnivals had boring old stuffed animals, but this carnival had dolls. Not just any dolls. Tim liked dinosaurs and the Titanic and butterflies. He wouldn't have said he liked dolls. But these dolls were amazing. They looked real. They had normal clothes, and many-jointed hands, and perfect little faces. Tim wanted a doll. "This carnival rocks," he told Ruth, and she nodded happily.

Tim and Ruth spent the evening in a whirlwind of color. They didn't stop until the sun was going down. They rode all the rides and played all the games. Spun in the Tilt-A-Whirl, laughed at each other's reflections in the funhouse. Ruth even got to ride a lion on the merry-go-round. And finally, Tim won a doll. It had a red shirt and a little belly and big, scared eyes. He stuck it in a back pocket.

It was nearly dark by then. Tim's hands were sticky. Ruth's mouth was smeared with chocolate. The lights on the midway flashed even brighter: red pink green blue gold. Music blared and blatted. They were getting tired. Ruth said, "I'm thirsty. Can we get more lemonade?"

Tim was thirsty too. Even though the sun had vanished behind the mountains, the sweat still trickled down his back. "Yeah—oh, wait, I don't have any money left. We should find Mom and Dad anyway. We're supposed to meet them at eight." His enthusiasm for the demolition derby had cooled. He didn't think that even Cousin Maynard's souped-up old derby car could compete with the carnival. The animatronic clown opened its mouth and called, Eight o'clock. HA HA HA. Eight o'clock. HA HA HA.

Tim pulled out his phone, but to his surprise, it said NO SERVICE. The shadows of the booths stretched long and black. The music and lights from the midway were starting to give him a headache. "No service. Weird. Let's go back to the entrance. This way."

Tim ducked behind the concessions to head toward the front gate, and Ruth followed him. But somehow they managed to turn left instead of right and found themselves walking down a darker path, where the lights and the noise were muted.

Suddenly Ruth grabbed his arm. "What's that?"

Tim was frowning at his phone again. "What?"

Ruth pointed. "Look! Wait, no—it's gone. It was yellow. It—looked kind of like—eyes. That corner there, behind that booth."

Tim looked where Ruth was pointing. Saw nothing. Just an old chocolate wrapper and some spilled popcorn. He huffed with impatience. "It was probably a cat, Ruthie. Or maybe you saw the lights from the midway. This isn't right, anyway." He craned his neck to see over the blocky shoulders of booths. Strange, he thought, how dark it was, the second you got away from all those lights. "What we need to do is just go straight, and when we get to the Ferris wheel, go left, and the gate should be right there."

They started off. But after a few seconds, Ruth stopped again. Tim turned around. "What's up?"

"Look at that," Ruth whispered. There was a building on their left. Tim hadn't seen it before. It wasn't lit up like the other buildings. Its windows were grimy and broken. A dim sign across the front said HAUNTED HOUSE.

Overhead, crouched on the roof, was a giant clown skeleton. Frizzy red hair topped a skull. A scarlet clown mouth was drawn around a huge, bony smile. It looked like a dead version of the clown with the clock on the midway.

Ruth stared up at the clown skeleton. "I don't like it."

"Oh, don't be a baby." Tim was peering with interest at the haunted house. The front door was shut, paint peeling. Yellow caution tape stretched across.

Ruth tugged his arm. "Let's go find Mom and Dad."

"Hang on. This place is cool. Think that door's locked?" Tim took a few steps closer.

Ruth was backing away. "Don't know, don't care. Come on."

A light flickered in one of the windows.

Tim said, "I want to look inside. Maybe it's a secret ride!"

"I don't want to." She grabbed his hand. "Come on, Tim, let's go."

"No, get out of here—go on, darn it. Go," muttered a breathless voice.

Tim and Ruth both yelped and spun around. A girl was standing in the shadow of the haunted house. It had almost sounded like she was talking to herself. She had curly hair and dark eyes. Had she come out of the haunted house? What was really in there?

A bunch of kids scream-laughed from the midway. They seemed strangely far away.

"I'm sorry, who are you?" asked Tim.

The girl's eyes widened. "You heard me? Can you see me?"

Tim stared. Maybe she was sick? Having an episode? He

said as gently as he could, "Um—yeah. Of course we can see you. Are you okay?" The girl was skinny. Her shoes were dusty. She looked wary. Alert. Maybe even afraid. Her eyes scanned the dusty ground, the black, square shadows.

The girl shook her head sharply. "It doesn't matter. You need to go. Right now. Go back to the lights. It's dangerous to get lost in here, do you understand?"

"I— What do you mean, dangerous?"

The girl didn't answer. Her eyes were on the shadows. As though she might see something there. Something bigger than a cat. She pointed to a narrow gap between the backs of two booths, where the lights of the midway showed clear. "Go that way."

Tim was getting nervous himself. Tugging Ruth's hand, he started to edge away.

Then the strange girl blurted a question, as though she couldn't help herself. "What day is it?"

They both stopped. "What?" Tim said.

"Please." The girl's hands were clenched.

"August seventeenth. Are you okay?"

The girl was breathing quickly, her eyes darting all around. "And where are we? What state, what county?"

"Rutland. Vermont."

The girl let out a sharp breath. "Thanks. Now get out of here."

Tim said, "Look, you don't seem okay. Can you— Is your mom here?"

The girl shook her head. "I— Go!"

Her fear was contagious. But Tim felt bad just leaving her scared in the dark. "Well, that's okay. You can come back with us. We'll find—someone. For you. Come on."

"No," the girl said. "I can't."

Ruth tapped his shoulder. In a small voice, she said, "Timmy? Timmy, look."

Tim followed his sister's gaze. Back into the shadows. This time he saw a pair of eyes. They didn't look like a cat's eyes. Then he saw another pair. And another. Three. Four. Yellow eyes all around. Tim and Ruth started to back away. But the eyes came closer. One step. Then two.

Then Tim saw faces. The faces that belonged to those yellow eyes.

Ruth screamed.

"Get out of here!" the girl cried. "No, not that way, don't—"

But now Tim was screaming too. Blind with panic, keeping a grip on Ruth's hand, he sprinted away from the eyes—

And found himself running right up against the wall of the haunted house. He spun around, tripped, and fell with Ruth beside him. She was whimpering. "Oh God," Tim whispered. "Oh please. Who are you, don't hurt us, don't . . ." He couldn't see the strange girl anymore.

A hand reached out. He had an impression of dead-white knucklebones, long fingernails. A dirty ruffled sleeve.

He tried to get away. Thrashed. Screamed. Beside him, Ruth was screaming too. Fingernails snagged in his shirt. The eyes bored into his.

And then Tim Jenkins stopped screaming.

1

Two weeks later

SUMMER IN EAST Evansburg, and a sun like a hot white eye glared down at the cracked and shriveling earth. It hadn't rained in weeks. Months. The April showers had come on time, but May was dry as dust, and June brought in a thick, sticky heat that refused to go away. The sun parched the new leaves as they opened, and made them curl up like caterpillars on their twigs.

July came, but the rain didn't. Families' wells went dry, so they had to truck in water, and the sticky air lay like a hot puddle in houses and never seemed to go, no matter how often they opened and shut the windows. The only people who enjoyed the heat were kids and the makers of creemees. And even for kids, riding bikes around town started to lose its appeal, with the sun glaring down.

Swimming holes were mobbed every weekend.

The East Evansburg swimming hole was on Lethe Creek. A cold green place in the stream where the water slipped under a covered bridge. Little kids liked to play on the rocks there. On really hot days, parents set up their chairs right in the water, dipping their feet and calling to their neighbors.

On a Saturday in late August, the heat lay on people's necks like a hand. Parents in chairs kept soaking their T-shirts and wearing them wet against the white-eyeball sun. Kids chased dogs into and out of the water. People shouted and people laughed.

Six parents sat with their chairs arranged in a tight circle, right in the water, so their bare feet stayed wet. Three of them were moms, and three were dads.

They weren't laughing.

"Coco won't talk to me," one said. Her blond hair was plaited down her back, and she wore a plaid shirt over her swimsuit, to protect her skin from the sun. Coco was her daughter. "But something's wrong. I just know it."

The man next to her had dark, sad eyes. He took her hand but didn't say anything. He'd had a daughter named Olivia, but she was dead. She'd died in a boating accident on Lake Champlain. Just that May. A few months ago. Sometimes he dreamed that she wasn't dead. Sometimes he dreamed that she was looking for him. But he knew those were just dreams. She was dead.

He loved Coco, though. Loved her almost as much as the daughter he'd lost.

"Brian won't talk to us either," Brian's mom said. Her swimsuit was orange, her expression serious.

"It's just—darn it—" another dad said. He had glasses and threw his head back when he drank his ginger ale. His son's name was Philip Greenblatt. "Something's wrong, but they won't trust us with it! They just say, 'No, everything's fine, Dad, I'm going to Brian's for a sleepover.' Or wherever. But they're all jumping at shadows. I *know* Phil isn't sleeping."

Coco's mom said, "Coco cries in her sleep sometimes. She's been having nightmares. I—she used to talk to me all the time, but now it really is like she doesn't trust me anymore." She rolled her drink between her hands without drinking it. The sun beat down on all of them.

"I'm worried," Brian's mom said.

"We're *all* worried," put in her husband.

"Especially since those two kids disappeared," Brian's mom went on. She lifted her hair off her neck. "Parents have a right to be worried, don't they? What were their names? Ruth and Tim? Just snatched right out of the Rutland fairgrounds. Awful."

13

They all exchanged dark looks. Behind them, most of the kids of Evansburg were splashing and yelling in the water.

Phil's mother said, "I have half a mind to keep Phil and Mikey home. When the fair comes here this year."

"Or at least keep a close eye," Coco's mom said.

Brian's mom said impatiently, "But whatever's bothering the kids—it started before this summer. It started with that field trip last October. Doctor says Brian's fine, but . . ."

"Maybe we should keep the kids apart?" Coco's mom said.

The rest of the parents turned to look at her.

She went on, haltingly. "If— Do you think they—that they—I mean, they're all good kids, don't get me wrong. And I know they're best friends. I was so glad to see Coco making friends when we first moved. But maybe they—I mean—sometimes it seems like they've built up this imaginary world together. No grown-ups allowed. And it—scares them, somehow? Coco was never a very imaginative kid—she liked books about flowers and insects, for God's sake—and now she wakes up in the night screaming."

Hesitant nods all around the circle. Brian's mom said, "I hate to say it, Zelda, but you might be right. I can't think what else to do, not unless they tell us—*something*. We don't have to be obvious about it, you know? Just keep the kids close to home until school starts. And maybe if anyone does pry it out of their kid, for God's sake, text everyone else. I hate, I *hate* not knowing what to do."

"We all do," Zelda said.

————

"What do we even *do* now?" Brian Battersby demanded of his two friends. He wanted to pace in frustration, but the three of them were clustered above the swimming hole, on a small rock ledge right under the trestles of the East Evansburg Bridge. There wasn't room to pace. His friends, Coco and Phil, were sitting with their backs against the struts of the bridge, their feet dangling. Above them was the shadowy span of the old covered bridge. The water below threw up white glimmers of light that speckled their hands and faces.

Instead of pacing, Brian stood restlessly, shifting from foot to foot. He was wearing green swimming trunks, his nose and shoulders striped pale with sunscreen. His expression, usually easygoing, was one of built-up frustration, his dark eyes narrowed. If it were a different summer, he'd be in the water, laughing, dunking, joking with a crowd of friends. But not this summer.

The bridge vibrated now and again when a truck or car passed overhead. The shrieks of six kids on a dragon floatie soared up from the creek under the bridge.

It was a beautiful spot. Cool. Quiet. The water was icy and clear, and the struts of the bridge half hid the three of them from the crowd at the swimming hole. This ledge had been the favorite sitting spot of a girl named Olivia Adler.

But Ollie wasn't there. Ollie was gone.

Brian glared down at the water. His friend Coco Zintner said, "For Ollie? We can't do anything but wait. You know that, Brian." Coco wore a purple swimsuit. Pinkish blond hair straggled damp over her neck, and her eyes were the same light blue as the August sky. The remains of sparkly polish spotted her bitten fingernails.

Brian said, "I know. I hate it, though."

"We all do," Phil Greenblatt said. He had a freckled snub nose and boy-band brown hair that fell into his eyes.

Brian sank back down on the ledge beside his friends. "Why'd Ollie do it?" he whispered. "She didn't ask us—she didn't ask us to help her or to try another way. She just— did it. Left us. *Chose to leave us.*"

Coco said, "Don't be mad at her. She did it to save her dad. Just like I would have done for my mom, or you for your parents. Maybe she should have talked to us, but Mr. Adler was *dying*, right there. She didn't have time."

"She should have trusted us," Brian said. He *was* mad at Ollie. He missed her and he was mad at her. Was that strange?

"She didn't want us to stop her," Phil said.

"We'd have found another way," Brian insisted.

Neither of his friends said anything. None of them knew if that was true.

"We'll get her back," Coco said instead, encouragingly. Coco was an optimist. "Remember what the letter said? *You have one chance to win her back.* Well, we're going to win, that's all. We'll get her back."

Brian said, "But *how*? She's been gone for months. Yeah, maybe the *smiling man* offered us a chance, but he's tricky. We don't know what that chance looks like. Maybe we missed our chance. Ollie's dad doesn't even remember what happened. No one remembers but us! Sometimes I think—that she really is gone."

His friends didn't answer. There was nothing to say. It was a conversation they'd had at least a hundred times. Brian leaned back against the cool stone of the rock face above the ledge and shut his eyes.

Abruptly, Coco said, "I dreamed about her last night." Both boys looked at her. Coco went on hesitantly, "She was trying to tell me something, but I couldn't figure out what it was. And then someone—someone I couldn't see—dragged her away. I woke up—I think I was screaming. Mom was there. She looked worried."

All three of them turned to look at their parents, sitting in chairs in the creek. The grown-ups seemed to be staring back at them: Brian's parents and Phil's, and Coco's mom, and Mr. Adler, Ollie's dad. Mr. Adler wore the expression of puzzled sorrow that never left his face in those days. It made Brian hurt inside.

All the kids glanced hurriedly away again. "Our parents look like they're plotting," Phil said.

Brian shook his head. "Can you blame them? We're acting certifiably weird. Have been for months. We need to chill them out somehow. Or my mom's going to keep me at home doing chores until school starts just so she can keep an eye on me."

The other two nodded, and they lapsed into silence. When Ollie first disappeared, they'd made all sorts of plans. Met up every day. Schemed, collected food, made emergency adventure packs.

But nothing had happened. Now they were just waiting.

Coco stiffened. "What's that noise?"

Both boys went still, turning their heads to listen. It was difficult to hear any stealthy sound at Lethe Creek on a summer day. There was the roar of the water to contend with, and the rumble of traffic going over the bridge, and the squeals and the laughter as half of Evansburg played in the stream. But Coco, Brian, and Phil sat still and listened hard, and after a few moments, they all heard it.

Furtive footsteps.

Coming nearer.

A rustling in the bushes.

Without a word, they got to their feet. The water rippled past, fifteen feet below. Phil looked ready to jump down and escape. His face had gone so white that his freckles and his sunburn stood out like brown and red ink. Brian didn't blame Phil for being nervous. They'd been hunted that May, after all. Hunted, and almost eaten. They'd run, they'd hid. They'd survived. But they'd lost Ollie.

Brian and Coco stayed put. Brian bit his lip. He was done hiding.

The footsteps got closer.

Closer.

And then, with a roar, something sprang out of the bushes.

Phil shrieked and fell into the water. Coco lurched backward too, although she didn't fall. Brian grabbed at whatever it was, only to feel bony limbs and hear a familiar, annoying voice yelling, "Gerroff, Brian, stop it, was just a joke!"

Brian let go and scowled down at Phil's little brother. Mikey Greenblatt shook himself and started laughing. Mikey was seven, and had a lot more freckles than Phil, but the same brown hair. "Hahaha, you should see yourself! I scared you, didn't I? Scared your face off!"

Brian was still breathing fast. Coco was still leaning on a strut of the bridge, panting. Neither of them liked being startled.

Phil was below them now, treading water in the creek. "Mikey, what was that?" he bellowed. "When I get back up there, I swear I—"

"Phil, don't yell at your brother!" his mother shouted from her place in the ring of chairs.

Coco snorted a laugh. "Yeah, you got us, Mikey. Don't you have anything better to do?"

Mikey said, "Um, no. Not when you guys scare so good. I mean, *really*, you should have seen your—" He broke off. His face changed. He was looking downstream. "What's that?"

Brian crossed his arms. "Oh no. Nope, absolutely not, you don't get us again. Come on, Mikey, jump back in the water and leave us—"

But now Coco was looking in the same direction. She held up one hand to shade her eyes. "Wait. Brian, what *is* that?"

Mikey said, "Is that a kid?"

"It's a kid." Coco's voice had gone strange. "Do you see, Brian? There, just between those rocks."

Brian followed her pointing finger.

Someone was running up the rocky creek bed. Sometimes on the bank, between the trees. Sometimes wading in the water. Brian saw a torn T-shirt. Bare feet. An open mouth. Wide, panicked eyes. And then he realized that the person was screaming. Screaming for all they were worth, but they couldn't be heard over the happy squeals of kids in the water of Lethe Creek.

2

"MIKEY, GO GET your mom and dad," Brian said.

"But I—"

"*Do it,*" Coco snapped. Mikey shut up. Coco had that effect sometimes. Probably because she yelled so rarely. Brian was already jumping. The quickest way off their ledge was to cannonball straight down into the water. Brian had a mean cannonball. He dropped like a rock. Heard twin splashes as Coco and Mikey hit the water behind him. And then Brian was swimming, ducking around the kids on their dragon floatie.

"Hi, Brian!" one of the girls called. He waved back without really stopping.

A few more strokes and his feet touched the rocky creek bed. Coco came splashing up behind him. He could hear Mikey's high, excited voice as he veered off to the right and hollered at the parents in the ring of chairs.

Phil popped out of the water beside Brian. "What's up, guys?"

Coco had gotten her feet under her; she pushed her hair out of her face and pointed.

Phil frowned. "Who is that?"

The kid was still running, slipping and sliding on rocks. Now that they were closer, they could hear his sobbing breaths. They hurried to meet him. "Help me. Help me, please," the kid gasped.

Coco said, "Oh my God. Isn't that—"

Brian had recognized the kid too. They'd seen his picture in the paper. His and a girl's. Brother and sister. Tim and Ruth. They'd vanished during the carnival at the Rutland county fair.

Phil said what they were all thinking. "Whoa. It's Tim Jenkins."

Tim hurtled the last few steps toward them and tripped. Brian caught him just in time. Tim smelled like he needed a shower. Tears cut the grime on his face. He clutched at Brian. "Don't let them find me. *Please.* Don't let them find me."

Phil said, "Hey, it's okay. No one's going to find you."

"Who is looking for you, Tim?" Coco scanned the river warily.

Tim whispered, "They'll eat you if they catch you. Or they'll hang you up. I didn't want to get hung up. But they did . . ."

"Who are *they*?" Brian asked.

Tim shook his head. "That wasn't what I was supposed to say. The man—he told me—told me to run. To run upstream. And I promised I'd say—what? Say something? I forget now. I forgot! He said he'd take me back if I forgot! Let them hang me up again!" Tim's voice got shriller and shriller.

"Who said? What man?" Coco whispered.

Tim's wild eyes darted from the hot rocks, to the rippling creek, up to the bleached-blue sky. "He was nice. But he scared me. I asked for Ruthie and he said no. I wanted to stay for Ruthie, but he pushed me in the water. Maybe I should try to get him to take me back. But I'm scared."

"What did you promise to say?" Coco asked. Her voice, if strained, was still calm. "What did he—the nice man—what did he want you to say? You need to try to remember, Tim. It's really important, okay?"

"It didn't make any sense."

"That's all right," Coco said.

Tim frowned. "'Need light.'" He scrubbed at his nose with a dirty hand. "And something 'bout keys. Three keys. Three. I remember three. Three words, for three keys. 'Ghost. Mirror. Gate.' That's what he said. And—" Tim gulped. "'Play if you dare.' He said that too."

Play if you dare.

"Tim," Brian said intently. "Where—"

But it was too late. There were shouts from behind him, crashing footsteps in the creek. Then they were surrounded by a wave of people. Mr. Adler was there first. "My God. That's Tim. That's Tim Jenkins. No—call the police, give him some air—"

But Brian hardly heard. He and Coco and Phil were staring at one another.

Brian whispered, "Ollie's close. Has to be. The *nice man*? That was the smiling man! *Play if you dare*? Who else could it be? This is it. Our chance!"

Coco nodded.

Phil asked, "But what does it mean? Need light? Three keys? Ghost, mirror, gate? I mean, *what*?"

Brian didn't know. Coco didn't look like she knew either. Tim had already been whisked off. "We need to ask Tim more questions," Brian said.

The other two nodded. They started wading toward the crowd by the creek. Tim was on the bank; Mr. Adler had put a big, dry towel around him.

"You don't have to say anything, son," Mr. Adler said.

Then he turned and called to the curious crowd: "Not right now. Back off, you guys!"

"Police are on their way. They're calling Tim's parents," Coco's mom said to Mr. Adler. There were tears in her eyes. "Thank God," she said to Tim.

Tim shook his head violently. "No. No—they're coming. They're coming! Please, you don't understand . . . They're coming for all of you. *They've got room for all of you!*"

Now Brian's mom was talking gently to Tim. "Hush. It's okay, son. Don't try and talk. Brian—give him some room, please."

Brian said, "Mom, we really need to talk to him. He knows something important."

"And he'll tell it to the police. Brian, he's terrified. Don't bother him now."

"But he—"

It was no use. Tim was surrounded by a solid wall of careful, caring adults, and none of the kids could get near him. Phil's parents were already packing up their stuff. They looked frightened. Maybe everyone was frightened. Tim had showed up out of nowhere. It was uncanny. His expression was uncanny. His eyes looked like holes burned in printer paper. No one knew where he'd been. Who'd kidnapped him. If they were nearby.

"We're getting you and Mikey home," Mrs. Greenblatt

said to Phil. "*Now*, Philip, there are enough people keeping an eye on that boy, and the rest will just have their cars blocking the police when they get here. You too, Mikey, stop rubbernecking. Come on, both of you. We're leaving." She was shooting wary looks at the creek, the trees, the bushes, the road.

There was no room to argue. Phil's parents nearly hauled him and his brother bodily up from the creek to the road. Phil only had time for a quick "Talk ASAP?" to Brian and Coco.

They nodded, and Phil was gone.

Then Brian's dad said, "We'll head out ourselves. Tell Coco goodbye, Brian."

Brian felt frantic. "What if Tim says something important?"

"Hopefully he does. To the police, and to his parents, and to a therapist. He's been traumatized, and pestering him with questions now is not going to help. It's the last thing he needs."

Brian tried again. "But—remember what he said? They're coming for all of you? *They've got room for all of you*? I mean—doesn't that sound like a warning?"

"Sure. He's had a terrible time. But it's okay. You're okay." And, misinterpreting the look on Brian's face, Brian's dad added, "*You're* safe, Brian. Don't worry. Your mother and I will keep you safe."

27

"Are you *kidding* me?" The question came out before he could stop it. Brian hated the way his voice cracked. "Keep me safe? You don't know what you're talking about. I'm not safe, *we* aren't safe. We haven't been for a while. I *have* to talk to Tim!"

Coco was shooting him worried looks. He closed his mouth before he said anything else. Even though his parents hadn't done anything wrong, it was hard not to be mad at them. To be mad at every grown-up who worried about ordinary things, while he and Coco and Phil carried around their fear, waiting all alone.

His mom stopped zipping up the cooler. "Don't you *dare* talk to your father like that! We don't know what we're talking about? Then why don't you tell us, young man? What do we need to be worried about? Huh? Tell us that, Brian!"

The answer ran through his head, so loud he was almost surprised his mom didn't pick the words right out of his brain. *Ollie's alive, somewhere. There's a—a person who's playing games with us. Game after game, and we don't know how to end it. We're scared he'll get us, we're scared we won't see Ollie again. I'm so freaking scared, Mom.*

But he didn't say any of that. Once, by accident, Mr. Adler had slipped with them into the smiling man's world. He had almost died. Brian would do anything to keep that from happening to his parents.

His mom pressed her lips together. She looked sad. "Get in the car, Brian. Right now. We're going."

Brian went. The last thing he saw was Coco's wide-eyed face. "Talk to you soon," she said.

He nodded.

The last thing he heard was the faint wail of police sirens in the distance.

3

TIM WAS SHAKING. Coco heard his teeth chatter, even though her mom and Ollie's dad loaded him up with T-shirts and dry towels. He wouldn't eat, even though they offered him his choice of baked goods from their cooler. He drank a little soda. And he shook.

"What happened to him, do you think?" Coco's mom whispered to Mr. Adler, in the breathless moment after people started to clear out and before the police sirens could be heard.

Mr. Adler shook his head. "Let's let him be, Zelda. At least until there's someone he trusts and a properly trained psychologist around."

Coco understood where Mr. Adler was coming from, but she really wished that Tim would—

Suddenly Tim blurted, "Ruth's still there. It was dark.

He wouldn't let me stay with her. I would have. The girl said she was sorry."

Coco's head slewed around. "What girl?"

"Coco—" her mother began.

Tim just looked blank. "Girl."

"Was she—what did she look like?"

"She looked sad. Then she looked mad. She was yelling at someone. But I couldn't see . . ."

"Was she—"

"Enough, Coco! Let's not stress him out, okay?" her mom said. Tim was shaking harder than ever. Ollie's dad and Coco's mom exchanged bleak looks.

"It's okay, Tim. You're safe now," Mr. Adler said.

"No!" Tim tugged on Mr. Adler's shirt, like a little kid desperate to make them understand. "You're not safe. No one is safe." He cringed into his layers of towel. "It's getting dark soon, isn't it? They come for you in the dark. They'll hang you up with Ruth."

A chill like a cold finger snaked down Coco's back. She glanced at the sky. The sun was tilting, but there was still time left until full dark—summer nights were short.

"Tim," she tried again. Both her mom and Ollie's dad gave her warning looks—*Why are you bothering him, Coco? We thought you knew better.* Coco ignored them. "I know you probably don't want to talk about it, but this is really important. *What* is coming?"

The sirens got louder.

She didn't think Tim would answer. Then—"They laugh when you scream. Their eyes shine in the dark. That's all I—" He shuddered. "I couldn't move. Then the nice man said I could go but I had to remember. Ghost, mirror, gate. You need light. Three keys, and *oh God*," His voice changed. "Is it going to be dark soon? Is it? They're coming! We have to hide. We have to hide!"

"Easy," Coco's mom said, trying to calm him. "It's okay. We're all okay."

But it wasn't okay. The flashing lights of the police cars reflected red and blue off the water. There was the sound of footsteps on the path from the road, and then Tim Jenkins started to scream. He screamed and he screamed, and so the police came running down through the trees to the creek with their guns drawn. That made him scream some more. There were two cops. One was youngish, and skinny. The other was older, and chubby.

Coco's mom snapped, "Put those things away, you're scaring him!"

"Oh my God," the older cop said. "I didn't believe it. That's Tim Jenkins."

The younger one holstered his gun. The older one kept his in his hand, looking at the moving shadows of the trees, of the water. "Whoever the kid got away from can't be far. What's he said?"

"Nothing that makes sense, Bill," Ollie's dad said soothingly. Coco was still getting used to how people in Evansburg all knew each other. "Look, just put it away, why don't you? Whoever it was is hardly going to try anything with all of us here, even if they are nearby. You're scaring him." Tim still hadn't let go of Mr. Adler. "It's all right, son," Mr. Adler said to Tim. "You're safe."

"What happened, Roger?" Bill said.

"Don't know. The boy appeared in the creek. Alone. Hysterical."

"The lights," Tim whispered.

Suddenly Coco understood. "It's your cars. He's scared of the emergency lights."

Both the older and the younger policeman gave her skeptical looks.

But unexpectedly, Coco's mom said, "She might be right. Wasn't he taken from a carnival? That has flashing lights too. It's residual trauma. Turn them off, for God's sake, and see if it helps."

"Now, listen, lady," began the older policeman, Bill. The younger one merely raised an eyebrow.

Coco's mom looked annoyed. "Don't *lady* me, Officer. I am a journalist for the *Evansburg Independent*, and I'm already taking notes for the article that will be on the front page tomorrow morning. So try turning off your lights for *thirty seconds* and see if he *calms down*."

They did. Tim stopped shaking. He lifted his head. "You're safe now," Mr. Adler said again. But Coco could see Tim Jenkins's face. He sure didn't look like he thought he was safe.

He didn't say anything else.

It was nearly dark by the time the three of them left the swimming hole. The police wanted statements. Bill, the older policeman, was salty and serious and kept touching the butt of his gun. The younger guy's name was Luke Fier, and he was nice. He took their statements. "Came running right up the river? Why do you think that was? Any signs of an unknown vehicle?"

"No," the grown-ups said.

"Saying a few odd things, though," Ollie's dad put in. "Something about keys. And he kept repeating three words: *ghost, mirror, gate*. Any ideas there?"

Officer Fier looked thoughtful. "None at all."

He took a statement from Coco too. "Kids see things that the grown-ups miss all the time," he said. "All right, tell me what happened in your own words."

Coco chose her words carefully. "Well, I was on the ledge just under the bridge . . ." She went through the story. But she left a lot out. Like: *I'm pretty sure I know who kidnapped Tim. I might even know who set him loose. It's the same person. The worst person you'll ever meet. I know these are the opening moves of a game—like an opening gambit in chess—but I don't know the rules.*

"Any suspects?" the policeman asked, breaking into her fast-running thoughts. The shadows were gathering by then. She couldn't see him properly anymore. Just the movement of his encouraging smile and his hand grasping the pencil.

Coco wasn't in the mood for jokes. "Why would you think I know a suspect? Tim disappeared in Rutland, didn't he? That's, like, fifty miles from here!"

"Never know. Thank you for your time. Evening, miss. Ma'am." Luke Fier sauntered away.

4

Three months before

THE CARNIVAL TRAVELED by train, and Olivia Adler traveled with it. She never knew where they were. The landscape flickered by. It was sometimes urban, and sometimes wild. Sometimes sunlit, sometimes ghostly. But there were never any landmarks she recognized.

One car of the train was Ollie's. That was the only part of the train she saw. It had a bedroom with a brass bed, a tiny bathroom. An old-fashioned living room with ratty velvet covers on the chairs.

She had an awful cold, in May, the first time she woke up and found herself on the train. Not surprising, since her last memory before that was of jumping, fully dressed, into Lake Champlain.

She woke up alone. The nightstand beside her held a neat pile of cold medicine, a glass of water, and a bowl of soup. Her throat hurt. Her head hurt. She drank her soup, went to sleep, woke up, found tea on her nightstand, drank that. Went back to sleep, woke up, and she was well. The bedroom had a chest of drawers. She found white dresses in it, neatly folded, with yellowing lace and a faint smell of dried roses, as though the dresses had been there a long time and belonged to someone else. She didn't put one on. She stuck with her grubby jeans, her purple hoodie. Tried the door to her bedroom.

It opened, and she found a living room on the other side. Old-fashioned as anything. Gas lamps instead of light bulbs. Chairs covered with moth-eaten brown velvet. Silky yellow wallpaper. A round, scratched table with lion-paw legs. A fire burning in the fireplace, even though May was too late in the year, really, for fires.

Ollie was staring into the fire when he appeared. The smiling man. He stepped through a door at the far end of the room. She knew him instantly. Strange, because if someone had asked, she wouldn't have known how to describe him. He swapped names, after all. He swapped faces. Fair hair? Well. Sort of. Pale eyes? Maybe, but they changed with the light.

However, his expression stayed the same. He always looked like he was enjoying a joke and only he knew the punch line.

"Hello, Olivia."

He'd saved her dad's life. He'd also kidnapped Ollie.

But was it kidnapping if that was the bargain they'd made? What did you say to someone like that? "Um—hi."

He gestured at the round table. It had a chess set laid out. "Would you like to play?"

She didn't move. She was trying to think. A million questions ran through her head. She asked the most important one. "Is my dad okay? Are my friends okay?"

"Yes."

"Where am I?"

"On a train."

"Where are we going?"

He put his head to one side. "Here and there. Do you want to play or not?"

Ollie swallowed. *You decided to do this, Ollie. You called him, you told him you'd do what he wanted if he saved your dad's life. And he did, and here you are. Are you going to start getting scared now? Maybe he'll tell you things, if you're clever. You don't even know where you are.*

"Okay. I'll play." Somehow, it seemed like the phrase meant more than *Yes, I'll play chess.*

"Wonderful." His smile was kind. Warm. That was the thing you had to remember about the smiling man. Sometimes his smiles were scary, and sometimes they were friendly, but they never meant what you thought they did.

They played chess every evening after that, at the

lion-paw table, sitting on the ratty velvet chairs. She didn't know for how many days. Two weeks at least. The train went on without stopping. Soon spring would be turning to summer back in Evansburg. The chess set was nice. Heavy pieces, of black and white stone. He was better at chess than she was, but he'd spot her a knight or a bishop. Then they were pretty even.

He liked to play chess. Genuinely liked it, Ollie thought. He liked games, and he liked figuring out people's weaknesses. Sometimes she wondered—and this was a strange thought—if he didn't have anyone else to play with.

Sometimes he joked, in a dry, malicious sort of way. Sometimes she even laughed. He knew strange stories. She wondered which ones were true.

The train chugged on, endlessly.

Her meals appeared on the round table in the living room. She never saw who left them. There was a bookcase in the living room. It had good books in it. She found *Alice's Adventures in Wonderland*, *The Phantom Tollbooth*, *Beauty*, *Coraline*. She wondered if there had been another kid traveling on the train who liked to read, or if the smiling man just had good taste in books. She would read by the window and watch the landscape outside. She saw graveyards sometimes. Gray trees. Shabby houses, and a square tower on a lonely hill. Once she saw a row of skeletons hanging from the same branch, bony feet stirring in the wind. She jerked back from the window, shivering.

Sometimes she wondered if she'd keep riding the train until school started, until winter break, until a year passed. Until she grew up. That thought scared her. She missed her dad. She missed her friends, her house, the smell of the woods. Her *life*.

But Dad's alive, she reminded herself. *It was worth it.*

Some time after she arrived—three weeks? She wasn't sure—Ollie moved a pawn and asked, "Does the train ever stop?"

The smiling man moved a knight. His abstracted gaze was on the chessboard. "It will stop tomorrow."

"It will? Then what happens?"

"You'll see." He seemed to know what she was wondering. He added cheerfully, "You'll be able to walk around. Won't that be nice?"

She almost didn't believe him. It seemed like the train had to stay in motion. Like a shark. Couldn't exist without the shifting scenery outside her clouded window.

But when she woke up the next morning, the train had stopped. It felt like there was something wrong with the floor at first. And then she realized that they weren't moving and ran to the window.

She was still in her bedroom on the train. She had to look around to be sure. She was. But now her window was fifty feet in the air, and she was looking out at a—glass castle? Her astonished gaze darted left and right. Not a glass castle—a mirrored funhouse. She saw a Tilt-A-Whirl. A Ferris wheel. Saw that it was summer. You couldn't mistake the yellow quality of the light. She'd gotten on the train in May. But now it was June, at least. And there was a carnival spread out at her feet. Laughter floated up to her window. People—families, ordinary families, with kids— were coming through the carnival gates.

Could she go out to them? Talk to someone? Find out where they were?

What day was it? How had the carnival gotten here? Was it on the train the whole time?

She tied back her cloud of corkscrewing hair and darted from her bedroom. A meal was waiting for her on the table in the living room, but she ignored it. She dashed to the far door. She'd tried it before, of course, but it was locked. This time the knob turned, and she found herself on a dusty landing, with a narrow staircase. She took the stairs downward two at a time. Came to another landing, with a cobwebby door opening off. A sign on the door said SCRAPS. Another time, she would have stopped to explore— she'd had no idea that any of this was here. Her rooms had been on a train car yesterday. But now all she could think of was getting outside, into the warm summer light, and talking to real people.

Another flight of steps, and then she came to a pair of doors. One said PARTS (BEWARE), but the other door said EXIT. She wasn't touching any door that said *beware*. Ollie tried the EXIT door, found it unlocked, and ran outside.

The smell of sugar and hot oil hit her nose. Sunlight felt wonderful on the back of her neck. Bright, blaring music came from unseen speakers. She turned to see the building she'd just left. The building looked like a carnival ride that had broken but was just kept around anyway. A sign in front said HAUNTED HOUSE. The façade was peeling. Cobwebs festooned the windows. On the roof was a huge statue of a skeleton. But it was a skeleton dressed as a clown. Its skull mouth was painted red. It wore a frizzy red wig. Red spots on its cheeks.

Another time it would have scared her, that she'd been living in a haunted house. But she was so happy to be out in bright daylight, and so eager to talk to someone. Anyone.

Ollie ducked between two booths and came out onto a vibrant carnival midway. People were pouring in through the gates. Kids spilled drinks in frosty cups, gobbled handfuls of chocolates. Smeared the candy on their faces. The Ferris wheel spun, sparkling.

One o' clock, HA HA HA, someone bellowed. Ollie

turned, saw that in the very center of the midway was a giant clown holding a clock in its two gloved hands. It had shouted the hour.

Carnies beckoned from each game booth, grinning.

I don't understand. Is all this—his? What is this place? The smiling man travels with a carnival? After everything— scarecrows and ghosts and monsters—he travels with a carni- val? It didn't seem like him. The carnival was beautiful. It seemed like fun.

Ollie reminded herself to be wary. The smiling man was tricky. And she hadn't forgotten his first question to her: *Would you like to play?* Maybe he'd been talking about chess. But maybe he hadn't been. And if they were playing a game now, she didn't know the rules.

She passed a merry-go-round, full of fantastic animals. Watched the Tilt-A-Whirl spin. Stared at the flags and tur- rets of the funhouse. Wandered through the game booths. There was archery where you had to shoot little mechani- cal dolls as they ran back and forth. There was a ring toss where you had to throw tiny life-preserver rings over more mechanical dolls half-submerged in a rippling black pool.

Ollie stopped at the ring toss, eyes on the attendant. Were the carnies all—his? His—what—employees? Did they travel on the train too? Were they his prisoners? His friends? She watched them mistrustfully. The carny at the ring-toss booth was tall and wide. He wore dull, nondescript clothes.

His face was pale, almost ashy. His teeth were yellowish. His hair frizzy. "Hey," Ollie said to him, but he didn't hear. He was beckoning some kids over.

They ran up. "Hey, how do you play this game?" one asked.

His buddy said, "Isn't it obvious? Throw the rings! What are you? Four? I want to play!"

The carny didn't say anything. He handed the boy three rings and pointed at the water, where the little plastic dolls bobbed. Then he pointed at the ceiling. Ollie looked up too. More dolls hung there. Beautiful dolls. Perfect in every detail. Painted eyes staring down. Prizes.

"Throw a ring on a doll, win a doll?" the boy demanded.

"But dolls are for babies," his friend said.

"Whatever. Look at them! I bet you could sell them to some girl for a lot of money. Or even a grown-up. On eBay. Stop talking, I want to throw. How much? Five dollars? Okay."

The boy handed over his money and threw. Didn't come close to a doll. Threw again. Didn't come close again. His freckled face screwed up in frustration.

Ollie had extremely good aim. She'd been starting pitcher on the softball team. She said, "Hey. Hey, give me the last one. I'll win it for you."

The boy ignored her. He rolled his shoulders, eyes intent on the target.

Ollie didn't like that much. She'd been trying for half an hour to think how to talk to someone, and now this kid was ignoring her. "Seriously."

He didn't react, just pulled his arm back to throw. Ollie, annoyed, got right in front of him. "Hey. I'm talking to you!"

The kid just blinked, stepped sideways, threw his ring. Missed.

Ollie stared at him. "Excuse me. Hello? Why are you ignoring me?"

No reaction. Not from the still-smiling carny. Not from anyone. Ollie snapped her fingers first in one boy's face, then in the next. Tapped the carny's shoulder. Nothing. *They can't see me. Why can't they see me?*

The thought trailed into a sudden, white-hazed panic. *Why can't they see me?* She remembered the sign that said, mockingly, HAUNTED HOUSE. And she lived there. *Am I a ghost? Is that it? Am I dead? Did I die in the lake? Did I? Did I?*

She bolted away from the ring-toss booth. "Hey!" she shouted. *"Hey!"*

But no one turned around. She snatched at hands, at shoulders, knocked a little girl's trucker cap clean off. No one reacted. *I am a ghost, I made a bargain with the smiling man, but it wasn't enough to save my life. I'm going to be haunting this carnival forever . . .*

She ran toward the front gate. It was a massive thing,

shaped like an open mouth. The vertical bars of the gate looked like teeth, with a huge keyhole like a gap in the middle. But somehow people still streamed through, talking, calling to each other, laughing, not a care in the world. Passing between the bars like they weren't even there. Maybe they were the ghosts? What did that make her? Ollie stared through the gate, pushed on the bars. She couldn't get through them. Beyond was—nothing. Just a roiling fog. She put an arm through the bars. Her arm vanished where it touched the mist.

It was too much. She wrenched herself back and fled again. Sprinted clear across the carnival, blind with panic. She shouted, to this person, then to that person. "Please! Please!" But no one answered. She passed the merry-go-round. The animals seemed to mock her with their flat plastic stares. She ran between the game booths, and the wide-eyed dolls seemed to peer down. But no one human, no one *real* even looked at her. She was still alone. In the middle of a crowd, she was still alone.

She forced herself to think, to stop running. Turned, feet tracking the dust, and went to the Ferris wheel. The carny didn't ask her for money. Didn't seem to see her at all. She got in one of the cars anyway and rode it up, staring down. Not at the carnival itself, but at its boundaries. At the world beyond.

But there was no world beyond. Just—mist. Just an

endless ring of fog, limitless, as though the carnival were the only real thing anywhere.

Ollie realized there were tears on her face, in her mouth. *I'll be here forever.* Then she closed her fists and said to herself, *Olivia Adler, stop crying. You can figure this out, but panicking won't help.*

She got off the Ferris wheel, scrubbing at her eyes. To her surprise, she saw the smiling man standing in the midway. He looked just like an ordinary person, out to enjoy a carnival: jeans, sneakers, a T-shirt with a rose-crowned skeleton that said THE GRATEFUL DEAD. "Not enjoying yourself, Olivia?"

She gave him a hateful scowl. Her face must have been snotty and tear-tracked.

He handed her, of all things, an old-timey handkerchief. Like no one had ever invented tissues.

She hesitated, and then she took it. Blew her nose. No point in being snotty. "Am I dead?" Her voice was more quivery than she'd have liked.

Both his eyebrows shot up. "Why do you ask?"

"Why do you think? No one can see me." She tried to hand him his handkerchief back.

He gave the damp handkerchief a look of distaste. "Keep it. You're not dead."

She went weak-kneed with relief—she hadn't known people did that, outside of books. A little giddy, Ollie said,

"I guess ghosts don't blow their noses." She wiped her face again.

"Perhaps you should ask a ghost."

She shook her head. She'd had encounters with ghosts, hadn't enjoyed it. "No thanks. Why can't people see me?"

The long summer afternoon was just starting to wander toward evening. Her exploration—and then her panicked sprint—around the carnival had taken longer than she'd thought. The moving Ferris wheel lit the smiling man's face in pulses of red and blue and green.

He shrugged. "You're behind the mist. Most of the people here aren't. So I suppose you are a ghost, in some ways. But not dead. Lemonade?"

She didn't want his lemonade. She craned to look at the carnival guests. "Can they see *you*? I'm sort of a ghost? Wait—what do you mean, *most* people?"

Instead of answering, the smiling man put out a foot and tripped a passing high schooler. The kid caught himself, staggering, turned back, and made a rude gesture. The smiling man's head was turned. Ollie couldn't see his face. But the high schooler went pale, backed away, stammered apologies, and then disappeared into the crowd. The smiling man turned back to Ollie. "Of course they can see me. If I want to be seen." He ignored her other questions.

"You didn't have to scare him," Ollie said.

"I like scaring people."

At least he was honest about it. "But people can't see me."

He was looking impatient now. "Do you want to stand here all night? I sincerely recommend the lemonade."

He knew she was bursting with questions, and he was going to amuse himself by not answering. The jerk. Or maybe this was the game. Figure out the carnival's secrets. Ollie tried to decide what to do. She could go back up to her room in the haunted house—*Oh my God, what's haunting the haunted house, if it's not me?*—or she could have lemonade and see if she could get the smiling man to tell her something helpful. "Is the lemonade poisoned?"

He snorted. "No."

"Is anything else poisoned?"

"Nothing will kill you, no." He started off down the midway.

That wasn't really an answer. Ollie stood there for a second, and then she followed him. He stopped at the concession stand. A word to the attendant, and he handed Ollie a frosty lemonade cup. He even took one for himself. "To reassure you," he said, and drank his.

"Like that's reassuring," Ollie said, holding her lemonade. "I bet poison doesn't work on you."

He said, "The lemonade will not kill you, make you sick, or turn you into a bird, a beast, or anything else, unpleasant or not. It is lemonade. Olivia, I will lie by omission all day, but I will never tell you anything that is untrue."

Oddly enough, Ollie believed *that*. She hesitated, and then she drank hers too. The lemonade was delicious. She made a promise to herself on the spot that she wasn't going to eat anything in this carnival that he didn't swear was safe.

The carnies, Ollie noticed, definitely saw *him*. They shrank away from him. He didn't seem to notice.

Six o'clock, HA HA HA, yelled the giant clown in the midway.

"Why are the carnies scared of you?" she asked. "Who are they?"

He shrugged. "They run the place. And of course they're scared of me. Plenty of people are." He was very matter-of-fact. "Do you want me to show you the carnival?" They were standing in the middle of a crowd of people, but no one jostled them.

"I already saw it."

"Have you considered that I know my carnival better than you do?"

Ollie drank more lemonade. A cool breeze filtered through the airless heat and cooled the back of her neck. "*Why* do you have a carnival?"

"I like my carnival."

Did he have a supplier? Did he buy cotton-candy sugar

and popcorn kernels from somewhere? Dolls for prizes? Or did he—magic them up somehow? Did he even do magic? What was magic? *Focus, Ollie.* She said, "I thought you only liked scaring people." Then she bit her tongue. Absurdly, her mother's voice in her head said, *That was rude, Ollie.* "Sorry," she added, a bit ridiculously. "I guess you like chess too."

He didn't look offended. He drank more lemonade. "People are complicated. Funnel cake? It won't poison you either."

"Is something terrible and scary going to happen? If you show me the carnival?"

He grinned at her. Outright *grinned*, like a big brother or something. "Not this evening."

"Promise?"

He raised his left hand. The first two fingers were exactly the same length. "I swear."

She thought, *He does keep his promises, right?* "Okay. Um—is the carnival—magic?"

He didn't answer. But his eyes flashed for a second, and she didn't think it was just the lights of the midway.

They set off. The shadows lengthened, and as the daylight dimmed, the carnival seemed to come alive. The crowd got louder. The lights got brighter. "What would you like to do first?" he asked.

"Beat you at ring toss," said Ollie instantly. Then she

bit her lip. It sounded like something she'd say to a friend. It was hard to play chess with someone for weeks without feeling friendly. Never mind what he'd done. Might still do.

But he just smiled. "You're on."

Sometimes he sounded old-fashioned, and sometimes he didn't. She gave him a curious look. "How old are you?"

"Manners, Olivia," he said.

They played ring toss, and his aim wasn't anything to write home about. Ollie won, whooping. "Take that!" she crowed.

He just laughed. But when the carny handed him a doll prize and he offered it to her, she eyed it and said, "No thanks." The doll was wearing ripped tights and a frayed miniskirt. A purple shirt. Its big blue eyes were thickly made up. Something about its perfect, worried face weirded her out. "Where do you get the dolls?"

"I have suppliers."

Ollie was dubious. "Is your supplier called Evil Dolls Inc.?"

He grinned and didn't answer. She threw an uneasy glance upward at all those plastic faces. "Do they come alive at night? That's it, isn't it? I bring it up to my room, it wakes up at night and tries to chop my head off? Well, no thank you."

"Really, you have the most extraordinary notions," the

smiling man said. "Chop your head off, indeed." Now he looked affronted, like a cat flicked with water.

Ollie said, "If it weren't for you, I'd be in Evansburg with Coco and Brian, riding my bike, and still you wonder why I'm suspicious. Could I try the Tilt-A-Whirl? Will it splatter me like a bug?"

He shook his head. "So suspicious. Use your head. What would people say if my guests got splattered?"

"I don't know," Ollie said. "What would they say?"

They rode the Tilt-A-Whirl until Ollie was dizzy. She wondered if he ever got dizzy. Certainly he didn't stagger off the ride like she did. She wished she hadn't eaten so much funnel cake.

He wouldn't go into the funhouse. "Why not?" she asked. She was a bit loopy from the sugar in the funnel cake. "Are you scared of the mirrors? Are you a vampire?"

"Guess again," he said shortly. He was frowning a little. He gave the big, mirrored building an odd look. Like he was uneasy. She wondered why he wouldn't go into the funhouse. "What next?" he asked.

Maybe, Ollie thought, *there's something in the funhouse that he doesn't want me to see.* She filed that idea away for later.

Finally the last of the sun left the sky, and Ollie found herself at the door of the haunted house, tired and breathless. "The carnival *is* magic, isn't it?"

He didn't answer directly. He said, "Olivia, you may do anything you care to, in the carnival, in daylight. But I warn you now, do not go out alone after dark."

Ollie looked around her and noticed then that the carnival was—very dark—the second you got away from the midway. She shivered. "What happens after dark?"

"Nothing that you will like. I promise you." He watched her carefully. "Unless you promised to stay. You'd be safe then."

She stared. "Stay? Here?"

"Yes. If you promised to stay, then you'd be safe. People would be able to see you. *You'd* see mysterious things. It would all be different. If you promised to stay."

"Forever?"

"Yes."

She was shocked to feel herself hesitate. Her mind was still full of the carnival's dazzle. "I wouldn't ever see my friends or my dad again, though."

"You'd see them," he said blandly.

"I would?"

"Yes," he said again.

She'd *see* them. She wanted to see them so badly. She was so lonely. She'd never have to go to school again. She'd travel with a magic carnival . . .

But Ollie remembered how he played chess. The way

his pieces slipped around the board, the way he never caught her king in the way she expected.

She said, "No thanks. I don't really trust you. So—let's stick to the original bargain, okay? My friends get a chance to win me back. I get a chance to go home."

His smile didn't waver. "As you like, Olivia." He opened the door to the haunted house for her. "Remember. Outside your rooms—it's dangerous after dark."

5

COCO'S HEAD WAS spinning and her sunburns were just starting to ache when she and her mom and Mr. Adler finally got in the car. Tim's third cousin or something, who lived in Evansburg, had gotten Tim's parents on the phone, and had driven, tires squealing, to the swimming hole. The cousin had run down to the water, yelling, "Timmy!" and eventually managed to pry Tim's cramping hands off Mr. Adler's shirt.

An ambulance showed up five minutes later. They were taking Tim to the hospital for observation. By then, there were people everywhere. But even with his cousin, even with a dozen grown-ups around, Tim didn't relax. He flinched at every moving shadow. Coco's last sight as they drove away from the creek was of his wide, panicked eyes and his lips mouthing the word *keys*.

They got into Mr. Adler's old Subaru and rumbled

down the dirt road from the swimming hole, leaving a trail of dust and a line of parked emergency vehicles behind them.

"Roger," Coco's mom said, "I'm worried. Whatever happened to that boy was awful. And they don't know who did it or how he just—ended up alone, walking up the creek bed."

"Must've escaped. Brave boy," Mr. Adler said.

Her mom nodded. "Will you— Do you mind staying over? Just until we know what happened to Tim? Maybe until they catch the terrible people who did it? I'll make up the guest bedroom."

"Of course," Mr. Adler said instantly. "I was going to suggest it myself."

Ordinarily Coco would have been delighted. She loved Mr. Adler. She'd never had a dad. Hers had gone away before she was born. And Mr. Adler was the best kind of dad. He was nice. He listened when Coco talked. He liked to bake. And knit. He was full of awful jokes that he laughed at louder than anyone. At least he used to joke. Before Ollie disappeared.

But she couldn't be delighted about anything just then. As Mr. Adler drove, Coco scanned the woods on either side of the road. She looked at the creek running alongside. She watched the sky, going from blue to green as the day dragged on. She thought of the ways that the smiling man could get you. With mist. With mirrors. With anything that made reality a little uncertain.

She wondered what had happened to Tim Jenkins.

She wondered what might happen to them.

But nothing bad happened at all. The Subaru rolled down the road and pulled up in front of the Adler house. It was an old farmhouse. Everyone called it the Egg because it was painted all the colors of an Easter egg. Although the paint was looking faded and shabby now, as though the house itself had been lonely since Ollie vanished.

Mr. Adler asked, "Want to come in for fifteen or so? I could make us a snack. And I need to pack a bag if I'm going to stay over."

"That would be great," Coco's mom said.

Coco looked at the sky again. She wanted to be home before dark. She didn't know if that would help, but it was an instinct. Home with the doors locked. Before the scary things came out. And then she could call Brian and they'd decide what to do. But there was still time, she thought. The summer days were long. "Okay."

They piled into the entryway, with its tiles of cracked slate, kicked off their sandals, and went into the big pistachio-green living room. Coco had always loved the Egg's living room. It was airy in summer and cozy in winter, full of light and heat from Bernie the woodstove. And of course, it smelled like Mr. Adler's cooking. But now there was dust on the furniture, dust on the floor. In the very last of the daylight, Coco saw threads of white in Mr. Adler's hair. He had a scar on the web of skin between his forefinger and thumb. Once or twice, Coco had caught him staring at the scar in confusion. Like he didn't quite remember where he'd gotten it.

He was peering into the fridge. "Milkshake? I know it's not really a good pre-dinner option, but it's *so* hot, and we could all use a treat. I could make chocolate, vanilla, peanut butter, or strawberry. Maybe mint chocolate chip too, but no guarantees about how it would come out."

"Yum. Strawberry, please," Coco said.

Her mom sighed. "For me too. If ever there was a day for it . . ." Suddenly she turned around and hugged Coco. "I'm glad you're all right. That was scary, what happened to Ruth and Tim."

"Oof," Coco said.

Mr. Adler started rummaging through ingredients.

Coco's mom pulled back. "Coco—look. I know you meant well, but we asked you not to frighten that boy— not to ask him questions—and you did. He got hysterical all over again. I need you to listen when I tell you to do something."

"I know."

Coco was going to add, *I'm sorry, Mom. It won't happen*

again. But then she hesitated. She thought, *Mom doesn't know why I tried to talk to Tim. If she'd known, she wouldn't have tried to stop me.*

They hadn't told the grown-ups anything. To keep them safe. Brian insisted on it, and Ollie too, before she disappeared.

But was that really what the grown-ups wanted? To be safe? Coco was pretty sure Mr. Adler would choose danger, even death, for the chance to get Ollie back.

What if I told them? Right here. Right now. I'm so tired of secrets.

Ollie would be angry. Ollie never wanted to tell the grown-ups. She did everything she could to protect her dad. Brian would be angry if I told too. Maybe even Phil. I hate it when my friends are angry at me.

You're thinking like a kid, whispered another part of herself. *This is more important than hurt feelings. Ollie's not here. What do you think is the right thing to do?*

"I know you told me not to ask Tim questions. But I had to," Coco said in a rush.

"Coco, what possible reason—"

"I had to!" Coco snapped.

Her mom drew back, startled. Coco heard Mr. Adler, on the other side of the kitchen island, stop slicing strawberries. "Coco—" Her mother took a deep breath. "Okay, you say you had to. Why?"

Coco sounded shaky, even to herself, as she said, "I'll tell you, okay? But you have to listen. You have to promise to listen all the way through." She paused. "Can we have those milkshakes first?"

————

"Ollie isn't dead," Coco began, when they were all sitting on the living room sofa with frosty drinks in their hands.

Mr. Adler went still.

Hastily, Coco went on, "She's missing. But she's not dead." She was holding her milkshake, hardly drunk, very tightly between her hot palms.

Mr. Adler opened his mouth, closed it again.

Her mom saw Mr. Adler's stricken face, and she looked angry. "Young lady—"

"She's alive! I *know* it. You promised to listen. You have to listen!"

"Coco—"

"No, Zelda. Wait. We promised we'd listen." Mr. Adler's voice sounded strange and fragile.

Coco said, "Thanks." Then she paused. Looked up. The sun had gone behind the trees on the other side of the creek. The light in the living room had dimmed. The parched yard outside was turning gray with dusk.

There was a shadow, thrown clear across the yard. A person's shadow. Coco saw two legs, a hand upraised. Saw the outline of—fingernails? A lumpy nose. A strangely twisted shadow. "Who's that?"

Mr. Adler turned his head. "What?"

"There—in the yard. There's someone out there." Coco was on her feet.

Mr. Adler said, "It's probably just the Brewsters. They're often over—"

"Just standing in the yard?" Coco felt her voice getting shrill. *"Not moving?"*

Mr. Adler looked at her face. "I'll check, if it would make you feel better," he said soothingly. He got up and went toward the French doors.

"No, wait. It might be dangerous," Coco said.

"Coco—" started her mother.

"Tim Jenkins was kidnapped by someone! What if they're outside?"

"Coco," her mom said again. She sounded like she was trying hard to be reasonable. Their abandoned milk-shakes made cold rings on the coffee table. "Why would Tim Jenkins's kidnapper be waiting outside the house?"

"Because I know who kidnapped him."

Both adults stared at her. "What?" Mr. Adler said.

Right at that moment, someone knocked on the front door. *Boom. Boom. Boom.* The daylight was almost gone. The shadow hadn't moved. The overhead lights flickered.

"No. Don't answer it," Coco said.

"Coco, no one is going to kidnap you," Mr. Adler said.

"You don't know, you're not *listening*—" The knock on the door came again.

"What's wrong with the lights?" her mother asked.

Mr. Adler shook his head. "Nothing. A tree must have blown down on the lines or something. I should get the door." He turned again toward the entryway.

Coco's mom yelped, short and sharp.

"What, Mom?" Coco demanded, spinning around. Her heart was going like a hummingbird's wings.

"Oh, I must have been— I thought I saw—a face in the window." Her mother was staring.

"What kind of face?" Coco whispered.

"Oh—honey, I must have been imagining things. It looked so pale. Strange eyes. Maybe a prank?"

Boom boom boom on the door.

"Enough of this," Mr. Adler said.

He reached for the handle just as Coco cried, "No, *wait*—"

But the door was already swinging open. And there was no one there. Except the porch light, flickering. Mr. Adler went out onto the porch. "Some joke. Of all the nights to—"

The shadow was gone from the yard. But . . .

"Wait! Do you hear that?" Coco said.

Her mom was looking exasperated. "What now?"

"In the house."

Both adults fell silent. In the stillness, Coco could hear the hot leaves rustle outside, and the sound of the creek.

And a sound from upstairs.

Thump. Creak. Another *thump*.

Coco held her breath. Someone was walking around upstairs.

Mr. Adler shut the front door. "Guys, stay down here, please. I'm not sure what's going on, but I'll just go see. Have your phones handy, and be ready to head next door to the Brewsters if you think that—"

Her mother interrupted, her voice sharp with anxiety. "You're not going up there alone. We should just call the—"

A massive crash cut her off. As though someone had pulled down a bookcase over their heads. All three of them jumped. Coco, heart pounding, whispered, "I—I think that was Ollie's room . . ."

Mr. Adler was already running for the staircase, wearing an expression of fury.

"Coco!" her mom shouted, but Coco was right on Mr. Adler's heels. No way was Ollie's dad investigating mysterious crashes without her. She heard her mom coming up behind them. To the end of the hall. Mr. Adler's hand was on Ollie's dragon-shaped doorknob. He was bursting into the room . . .

Silence. Stillness. Mr. Adler just stood in the doorway.

Coco's mom said, her voice surprisingly small, "Roger? Is everything okay?"

He didn't answer.

Coco peered around Mr. Adler.

The room was a mess. Stuff was scattered on the floor. Ollie's plushies had been torn open. Her novels lay broken-spined, like dead birds. The bedding was thrown back and ripped down the middle.

But there was no one there. The room was empty, except for the mess on the floor.

The window was open. Coco ran across the room and looked into the blue-gray dusk. Nothing. Just the rustling of the sugar maple outside Ollie's window, and beyond—was that movement? A scuttling, as though someone was sneaking away. But maybe she'd imagined it. The street was still.

Mr. Adler stumbled into the room like a sleepwalker. He knelt and picked up a picture of Ollie and her mom. It had been on Ollie's nightstand. The glass was broken in the frame. He tilted it and brushed off the glass, very gently. He didn't say a word.

"Oh, Roger," her mom said. "I'm so sorry."

"Who would have done this?" Mr. Adler whispered. "Who *could*?"

"Were they—looking for something?" Coco's mom asked tentatively.

"I don't see why. There was nothing valuable in here at—"

Coco felt like her heart was going to stop. Coco could think of one thing of Ollie's that the smiling man might want. Just one. But it wasn't in Ollie's room. It was—

"Mom?" she whispered, in such a strange voice that her mom and Mr. Adler both whirled around to face her. "We have to go home. We have to go back to our house right now."

"Honey, why? Honey, are you okay?"

"Because—I'm pretty sure I know what—the person who did this—what they were looking for."

"What was it?" Mr. Adler demanded. "And where?"

"That's just it. It's not here." Coco swallowed hard. "It's in my room."

6

BEFORE SHE DISAPPEARED, Olivia Adler had owned a wristwatch. It wasn't a smartwatch or anything. It was an old-fashioned digital watch. It had a bulky face, a built-in compass, and an altimeter.

Ollie's mom had it with her when her plane crashed. It was banged up, with a cracked face. Ollie always kept it close. Until she gave it to Coco in the minutes before she disappeared.

Coco always kept it close too. But she'd left it at home that morning, when they went to the swimming hole. Mr. Adler might see it and wonder how she'd gotten it. And there was a deep-down part of herself that complained, *I just want one normal summer day. Just one where I don't have to think about lost friends, or ghostly wristwatches, or danger.*

"Careless," she muttered to herself all the way back

into town. She and her mom lived on Bank Street, five blocks from Phil. "How could I be so careless?"

Coco loved their house. It was small and neat and had phlox and sunflowers growing in the yard. But she hardly saw the yellow front door, hardly saw anything, until she hurtled up the stairs and stopped in the doorway of her bedroom.

It was a mess.

"Oh my God." Her mom was right behind her. "Coco, how did you know? *Coco?*"

Coco's rug was covered with torn paper, stained with color from her beloved sketching pencils, lying broken. Her walls were smeared with smashed-open paints.

But Coco hardly saw any of that. All she saw was the desk drawer where she'd kept Ollie's watch. The drawer that was hanging open. She felt inside the drawer, but she already knew what she'd find.

The drawer was empty. Ollie's watch was gone.

Ollie's watch wasn't ordinary. It told them things. Important things. Ollie thought that a bit of her dead mother lived in that watch. And Coco had lost it. The one thing that might have given them an advantage. And she'd decided, on this one day, *carelessly*, to leave it at home . . .

"Coco?" her mom whispered, coming across the floor. "I know you're scared, honey. But this is serious. Do you think you know who did this? How did you know they would come here?"

Coco dashed the tears out of her eyes. She'd beaten the smiling man once. She wasn't going to let him win this time. Not in a million years.

"Let's go back to the living room," she said. "I'll tell you." She firmed her lips. "I'll tell you everything." She looked her mom straight in the face. "I really need your help."

Her mom studied her for a moment. She looked strangely relieved. Then she nodded. "Okay, hon. I am so, so glad that you said that. You can tell me anything. But first we're calling the police. We need to report the break-in."

———

The police came and went. Different officers this time. They took some pictures, looked around, nodded, left.

Mr. Adler had stayed back to wait for the police at the Egg while Coco and her mom raced home. After those officers had gone, he came into town. Coco was glad to see him.

He made pasta salad. "Too hot for hot food," he said. When he put the plates down at the table and they all sat, Mr. Adler fixed her with a serious expression. "Coco, keep on with what you were saying earlier. Before we discovered the break-in. How did you know the thieves would come here too? Does this have to do with what you were telling us?"

"Yes, hon. Can you tell us now, please?" her mom added.

Coco looked down at her pasta salad. She could smell the olive oil and sun-dried tomatoes. Delicious. She had no appetite at all. "Yes, it does. Here goes."

Coco started talking. She didn't stop for an hour. Neither adult interrupted. Her mother tried to say something once or twice, but Mr. Adler put his hand on hers, and she stayed silent.

Finally, Coco finished, "And then Ollie was gone. Not dead, but gone. And we got to shore. And neither of you remembered."

Both adults stared.

"And you still don't remember," Coco finished.

Her mother looked worried. Coco couldn't figure out Mr. Adler's expression. Finally, she couldn't stand it anymore. "Okay? Say something?" She hated how her voice came out small and squeaky when she was nervous.

"I don't know what to say." There was a worried line between her mother's eyebrows. "Coco, if this is a prank, it is an extremely hurtful one."

Coco felt like crying. "Mom, this is me! Have I ever played a prank? Ever? In my whole life? Never mind a completely maniac prank where I mess up people's houses—mess up my own room! And lie about someone I love! Why would I do that?"

"I don't—" Her mom looked a little helpless. Mr. Adler still hadn't said anything. Coco noticed that he was rubbing the scar on his right hand again.

In a strange voice, Mr. Adler said, "You think Ollie's alive."

"I *know* she's alive."

Mr. Adler went on in the same slow, puzzled voice. "And that—she's been kidnapped?"

"Sort of."

"By the same person that kidnapped Tim Jenkins."

Coco was more sure of herself there. "Yes."

"But somehow we—your mother and I—don't remember any of this—these things that happened to you."

Mr. Adler didn't believe her. Coco despaired. He wouldn't help look for Ollie. She'd tried, and she'd failed. Sadly, she said, "No—you don't remember. He's—I guess he's magic, in a way."

"Magic," Mr. Adler said.

It sounded unbelievable, even to Coco. "Yes." Her voice came out small.

"Coco . . ." her mother began, a warning note in her voice.

But Mr. Adler interrupted. "Coco, say I believe you. What would you want us to do?"

"I— Roger, surely—" Coco's mom spluttered.

Coco felt a ball of disbelieving hope rising like a sun inside her. "We need to visit Tim Jenkins. We need to find out what he knows. That's step one."

Mr. Adler nodded. He said, very simply, "Okay. We'll go and try to see Tim Jenkins."

Her mother broke out in protest. "Roger, please. You can't be serious. This is—the kids have been—this is clearly what the kids have been *frightening themselves* with for the last year, and we shouldn't encourage—"

"Coco has never lied to us. Have you, Coco?"

Coco shook her head, eyes still fixed on him in word-less hope.

"Well, then," Mr. Adler said, as though that solved that. "And this is the first time she's trusted an adult with her story. Isn't that so?"

Coco couldn't speak. She nodded *yes*.

"I think your mom and I both want to be worthy of that trust, Coco. If you need to visit Tim Jenkins, then that's what we'll do."

Somewhat to Coco's surprise, her mom agreed. "All right. But I don't know how we'll get in. There'll be national media for sure: a proper circus."

Coco said, "Well, Mom, you are a reporter."

Her mom stood up and started clearing plates. "We'll give it a try, then. Tomorrow morning."

"There's not much time—" Coco began.

But her mother fixed her with a gimlet eye. "A kidnapped child popped up alive in Lethe Creek. We had our houses broken into, and you think there's a kidnapper who has his sights on you too—and that he's *magic*. I don't know what to think, but I know that's enough for one night. We're washing up, checking the locks on the doors, and going to bed. I'm making you up an air mattress, *not* in your bedroom. And that," said her mom, in a tone that Coco knew was not be argued with, "is final. Finish your supper now. We're starting on dishes."

Coco picked up her fork and discovered that she had an appetite after all. Her heart felt lighter than it had in a long time. She was right to have trusted them. It felt good to trust people. It did.

She hoped Brian wouldn't be mad.

7

AFTER A FEW days, the carnival closed up, just like a real carnival would. But Ollie never saw anyone packing it. No one took down the rides. No one put the doll prizes into a box or onto a truck. Certainly the carnies didn't do any work. Still less the smiling man. The thought of him packing dolls into boxes almost made Ollie laugh.

She just woke up one day, and her bedroom was in a train car instead of the top of a haunted house. The train was chugging along just as though it had never stopped. Ollie looked out and saw scarlet trees on a steep-sloped hill, brilliant in pale sunlight. And then the train plunged through blacker trees, with small blue lights between them. Ollie didn't know what to think. She picked up *Alice's Adventures in Wonderland* and sat by the window without reading it. She felt like a child's lost balloon, drifting.

After five days—was it July by then? She wasn't sure—the train stopped again. The carnival opened up, under a different summer sky. The gate was still locked to her, the mist still outside. Ollie explored, but failed to find anything useful. She didn't even know what she was looking for.

She went through the carnival systematically that time. She rode every ride, played every game, explored every nook. Went through the funhouse, tried tapping the mirrors. Nothing. Tried talking to every carny. None of them replied. None of them, she realized, spoke at all. As far as she knew, they couldn't see her. They just smiled at people and gestured toward the games.

Once Ollie saw a boy fail to win a doll in the bow-and-arrow game. The boy tried to grab one anyway, reaching stealthily while the carny had his back turned. But the carny turned around. A large hand closed on the neck of the boy's shirt.

Ollie couldn't see the carny's face, just a finger wagging. But the boy's eyes widened. He wrenched himself away and bolted. The carny turned back to the other guests, smiling. When Ollie went looking for the boy, she couldn't find him.

"Do people disappear from your carnival?" she asked the smiling man, three nights later. The train rocked evenly down its track once more. The soft clacking of its wheels was a constant noise in the background.

He moved a piece. Considered the board. "People disappear from everywhere." He did not sound interested, even though Ollie knew for a *fact* that he made it his business to disappear people. It annoyed her.

"What happens to them?" she pressed.

"Who knows?"

She ground her teeth. "People who disappear from *the carnival*—what happens to them?"

"They don't disappear."

"No?"

A smile. "Not exactly, no."

"What do you mean *exactly*?"

But he wouldn't answer the question. Ollie was getting better at chess. She beat him that night, and he'd only spotted her his bishops.

She tried more questions, after he resigned, toppled his king, and got up to say good night. "Where does the gate to the carnival go?" she asked.

"Through the mist," he said.

"It's locked."

"To you, yes." She knew he was enjoying himself, giving her half-answers or no answers. *Where's the key? Where's the key to the front gate? Would that let me out?* The question was loud in her brain. He looked as though he knew very well what she wanted to ask. Ollie said, carefully, "Is there any way you would tell me where to find the key to the front gate?"

He said promptly, "Promise to stay forever, and I'll tell you everything."

"No," she said.

"Then good night, Olivia."

She racked her brain, trying to think of a next move. Not a chess move. A move in the other game. *He promised that Brian and Coco would have a chance to get me back. But I have to be ready to help them. I have to know more.*

———

They next time they stopped, Ollie decided that, since she wasn't learning anything from the carnival, she'd explore the haunted house instead. A little nervous, she went down to the first landing below her rooms. To the door that said SCRAPS. She wasn't ready to try the door below that. The one that said PARTS (BEWARE).

She pushed the door open. Stood in the doorway. Felt her stomach churn.

The room was full of dolls. Parts of dolls. Whole dolls. Old dolls, with old-fashioned clothes. Punk dolls. Kid dolls. Doll eyeballs and doll hands. Tier after tier of them. All the dolls seemed to stare at her. And all of them, however they were dressed, whatever their faces looked like, wore the same expression of wide-eyed terror.

She couldn't bring herself to go into the room. The dolls' faces made every hair stand up on the back of her neck. She imagined the door swinging shut, being alone in there, the dolls coming to life, burying her in a wave of plastic. Small biting mouths . . .

She backed hastily out of the doll room and shut the door. Went down a level and put an unsteady hand on the doorknob of the PARTS (BEWARE) room. Stood there hesitating. Wondered what could be in there, and if it was worse than the dolls. Probably. Why else would it say *beware*? She took a deep breath . . . and then she turned left and went outside.

What do I do now?

She couldn't get the thought of the front-gate key out of her head.

She searched again, but she didn't find anything. No clues. Just people who couldn't see her, the rides, the games, and sometimes the smiling man. Sometimes, during the day, he'd talk to her. Or she'd see him talking to people in the crowd. When she crept close enough to hear, he was always being charming. Joking. Laughing. She wondered if anyone but her saw through his jokes, or was afraid of his laughter.

Every night, after dark, she peered out her window,

trying to understand what made the night different. But all she could see was a blaze of light and, occasionally, a strangely twisted shadow. Finally, she thought in desperation, *Whatever he says, I need to go out and see the carnival after dark.*

She was scared to do it. But she wasn't learning any of the carnival's secrets by day. Maybe he'd just warned her off the night because that was when she'd get some answers.

So one night, after she lost their chess game—she'd been far too nervous to concentrate—Ollie gathered her courage and crept down the stairs. It was quiet and dark in the windowless stairwell. She tried not to look at the SCRAPS sign as she went by, or think of the blank-eyed ranks inside. Her nerves twitched at every creak. She paused again on the ground level, next to the PARTS (BEWARE) door, listening. But she heard only deathly silence.

Ollie slipped as quietly as she could out into the hot summer night.

She wondered if the smiling man would come looking for her. She wondered what he'd do. But she *couldn't* just sit in her attic any longer, waiting for something to happen. She tiptoed toward the midway. The sound of the crowd was even louder at night, but the music was different. It was high, wild, sour, *something*. A minor instead of a major key.

Here goes, Ollie thought to herself. She took a cautious step onto the midway, keeping to the shadows. She didn't know what to be afraid of.

She stayed in the shadow of the concession stand, trying to observe without being observed. Her first thought, strangely, was *wow*. If the carnival by day was beautiful, the carnival by night was wondrous.

The night was clear; the black-velvet sky made the perfect backdrop to the arcs and drips of light from the rides. The mirrored funhouse shone like water; the slow rotation of the Ferris wheel was mesmerizing. The music was the kind that made you want to dance. She didn't see anything obviously dangerous.

Someone, passing, gave her a strange look but kept walking.

Ollie didn't register it at first. But then she realized. *That girl saw me, she saw me, she . . .*

Ollie lurched into the light of the midway. People were everywhere. She grabbed the shoulder of the first boy she saw. "Hello," she said. "Hello, can you see me?"

The boy stared through her, moved on.

She'd been wrong. People still couldn't see her. Tears pricked Ollie's eyes. *But that girl saw me. I could swear that girl saw me.* She turned her head, looking. The girl had been hard to miss. Black, ripped tights, a frayed miniskirt.

Sleeveless purple shirt. Wary blue eyes, made up dark. Her appearance prodded something in Ollie's memory. She scanned the midway. Raucous laughter floated down from the Ferris wheel.

Someone caught her arm, turned her around. Ollie yanked away, expecting the smiling man, expecting him to be angry. But it was the girl again. The one in the frayed miniskirt. Even her face was weirdly familiar. But from where . . .

"Can you see me?" Ollie whispered. At least, she started to say that. She only got the first word out.

The hand on her arm pinched, a furious grip—and the girl bent down to hiss in her ear: "They've seen you. They're watching you."

Then the girl vanished, just like that, into the crowd.

Ollie shrank back into the shadows. It was hard to see. The lights were so bright, and they flashed so quick. A kid lost his ice cream and started to cry. Two high school kids were kissing, with drool. A pair of grandparents were smiling benignly at all the happy chaos on the midway.

Then something scarlet, and yellow, and white flashed past her eyes. Ollie blinked, looked again. Saw the carny from the ring-toss booth.

She'd never completely understood the carnies. The smiling man wouldn't say much about them. "The carnies never talk," Ollie had observed once, leaning on the lion-pawed chess table.

"They do occasionally," he replied. "Do you always feel the need to lean on the furniture? You are rattling the pawns."

She wished he wouldn't say things like that. Perfectly normal things. It made it hard to be wary of him. "When?"

"When what?"

"When do the carnies talk?"

"When addressed, I imagine. Do you want to play chess or not?"

"No, they don't. I've tried. I haven't heard them talk to anyone else either."

"One of the world's mysteries, I suppose." He was absolutely maddening. "If you will not pay attention to your bishops, Olivia, this game will be shorter than the last one."

They had gone on playing chess.

Ollie had definitely been *wary* of the carnies. They were his, after all. Part of the carnival. But she'd never been *scared* of the carnies. They were easy to overlook. They seemed like so much furniture, colorless furniture, in all that vibrant chaos.

But now . . .

The *colors* were the first thing she noticed. It was like

someone had wiped the ring-toss carny clean. Brightened him up. Dull, frizzy hair had turned scarlet. The pasty face had turned white. His nondescript clothes were now violently spotted, in a sick-making whirl of colors. Huge red shoes.

It's a clown.

But there was something off about this clown.

Its eyes gleamed yellow, over a bulbous red nose. Its mouth was a vast scarlet gash. And the clown was watching her. It was unmistakable, the way it was watching her. The way a cat watches a bird.

Ollie heard a footstep at her back. Looked down. Saw a giant red shoe in the dust. Smelled something sickly sweet, like candy, but with a whiff of rot.

She lunged forward, rolling in the dirt. Felt a wind at her back, as though someone had swiped at her hair and missed. She scrambled to her feet. Another clown was right behind her. It put its hand to its mouth and giggled.

Its nails were sharp.

So were its teeth.

Ollie bolted, pushing through the oblivious crowds. Stumbling, she strained to see over people's heads. How many were there? Were all the carnies clowns at night? She tried to remember the number of booths, the number of rides. But her brain was a white, scared blank. She thought of hiding in the funhouse, imagined being chased down mirrored halls, with her reflection and her pursuers' echoing endlessly. *No.* The Ferris wheel? Trapped in a car, while they waited below? *No.*

Get back to the haunted house? She tried, darting around the concession stand. Skidded to a halt at the sight of another clown. It gave her a finger wave, blew her a kiss.

Its teeth caught the light when it smiled.

Ollie thought, *Maybe I can lose them in the crowd.* She slipped back onto the midway. But suddenly, yellow eyes seemed to be everywhere. Coming nearer and nearer. A stitch was forming in her side. She was near the main gate. The white mist outside seemed to mock her. She tried to get through the bars, couldn't. She turned back.

Now the clowns had formed a loose semicircle around her. One of the clowns licked its lips. Two of them put their heads together and giggled. Another one was clapping its sharp-nailed hands excitedly, like a little kid.

She was trapped.

Then a girl's voice yelled, "Hey! Hey! Ugly!"

It was the girl in the miniskirt. She was behind the semicircle of clowns. She looked as terrified as Ollie was.

Two of the clowns turned toward the sound. Ollie threw herself between them, and they were just distracted enough for her to stutter-step, dodge a swipe of yellow nails, and get clear of the tightening semicircle. Behind her came a chorus of hisses.

The girl and Ollie ran between two rides, then ducked left, into the deep shadow below the Tilt-A-Whirl. They stopped there, breathing hard. "Who are *you?*" each girl said simultaneously.

After a startled pause, the stranger said, "I'm Morgan. Why aren't you hanging up?" Her voice was almost angry.

"I'm Ollie. I— What?" *Where* had she seen this girl?

"In the booths." Morgan sounded impatient. "There's only one of us down at a time. That's the rule. You're different. Why?"

Ollie stared. "Hanging? In the booths? Like the prizes? The dolls?" Her skin felt like it was trying to crawl off her bones. Wildly, she scanned the shadows. "The dolls are—?" Suddenly she knew where she'd seen that miniskirt, that makeup, those frayed tights. That face. "You," she whispered. "Was it you? You were a doll. At the ring-toss booth. I—won you." She felt sick. "The dolls are people, aren't they?"

"Yes," said Morgan.

Ollie tried to marshal her whirling thoughts. "But you—you're—not a doll now."

"Are you dim? We get let down. The clowns have to hunt."

"Hunt?"

"Yes. Mostly they hunt one of us. A doll gets let down, is turned human again, and runs as long as they can."

Ollie shuddered, imagining a whole night running from those huge shark smiles.

"Or sometimes, if a kid gets lost, takes a wrong turn—I don't know how it works—suddenly the clowns can see her. Or him. The clowns hunt her down. It's dangerous for kids to get lost in this place after dark. But you're not a lost kid. You're not a doll. Who *are* you?"

Ollie could barely speak. Part of her felt—was that *betrayed*? She knew the smiling man was bad. It was just hard to remember how bad he was when he was buying her lemonade and making her laugh.

"What happens if they catch you?" she whispered.

Morgan gave her a look like she was being unforgivably slow, and waved an impatient arm to the rows and rows of carnival prizes. Ollie thought she might be sick.

"We need to move," Morgan said hurriedly. "Do you know where the key is?"

Ollie's dazed brain could hardly grasp this. "The gate key?"

The girl grabbed the front of Ollie's shirt. "No! You can't just find the gate key. You need the first key."

"What's the first key?"

Before Morgan could answer, they both heard the

scraping footstep of a giant shoe in the dust. Ollie bit back a scream.

Morgan grabbed her hand, and they ran again. Careening between shadows and lights, ducking between carnival guests, they finally pulled up in the shadow of the Ferris wheel, crouching nearly under it. "They're—they don't quit. But they're not *that* smart," Morgan said. "You don't know about the keys, do you? You were never a doll. Who *are* you?"

Ollie whispered, "I'm no one. I just—I made a bargain with the smiling man. But part of the bargain was that my friends had to have a chance to save me. Maybe they couldn't save me, if I were a doll? I don't know. How did you get here?"

Morgan ignored the question. She said urgently, "So you—what—live here during the day? You've been around the carnival a lot? You know where stuff is?"

"I— Yes?" Ollie said. "I know my way around. But only by day."

Morgan's eyes were intent. "I've never explored. Not since my first time here, when the clowns got me. When they let you down, you're just trying not to get nabbed. Look, Ollie—the first key's in the place where the dead dolls go. That's what they say. But no one knows where it is. When the clowns nab you, they just put you back up."

Ollie licked her lips. "I know where that is," she whispered.

Morgan stared back. "Really?"

Ollie nodded.

Morgan jumped to her feet. "Let's go, then!"

"No," Ollie said. "Tell me about the keys first. I need to know everything."

Morgan looked like she might yell with impatience. But she forced out, "There are three keys. You need the first key to get to the second key. The second key to get to the third key. And the third key opens the front gate. If the front gate ever opens . . . well, that's it. Everyone goes back home. Back to their lives, like we never left. Like this was all a dream." Morgan's voice was heavy with longing. "But you can only find the keys at night. When the—the clowns are hunting. Those are the rules."

"Okay," Ollie said, trying to process all this.

"Now," Morgan said. "Where do the dead dolls go?"

"This way," Ollie said. "The haunted house."

"I'll follow you."

They ran together. Kept to the shadows, watched the midway. Stayed low, zigzagged. Once or twice, Ollie saw the white clown faces in the crowd. But they looked puzzled. They weren't smiling. Ollie and Morgan got to the haunted house unseen.

"Shouldn't one of them be guarding it?" Ollie asked. "There were three earlier. Could it be a trick? A trap?"

"I don't know," Morgan said. "They're not tricky, usually." There was a tremor in her voice. Ollie wondered where she'd come from. How she'd wound up in the smiling man's carnival. If she had a family looking for her. "But we should still go in," Morgan added. "Before they see us. Unless you have a better idea?"

Ollie didn't. She nodded, trying not to think of the gallery of faces in the doll room.

The two girls darted across the open space, through the front door, past the door that said PARTS (BEWARE). The stairs led up into blackness. Ollie felt Morgan breathing faster and faster. "It's so dark in here," Morgan whispered.

Ollie felt for Morgan's hand, took it. The older girl's fingers were deathly cold. "Come on. Just be careful of the steps."

They crept up the stairs to the door that said SCRAPS. Ollie groped in the dark for the handle, found it, pushed it down. The door opened with a shrill *creak*. Both girls froze, listening. But there was no one there.

They slipped into the doll room.

The cobwebby windows let in some moonlight, some carnival light. But the light wasn't stable. It pulsed. It flickered. It washed the room with different colors, it lit the dolls in pieces. Their rigid faces, their open eyes. Their broken limbs. The pieces on the floor. Morgan turned away, a hand over her mouth.

"It's okay," Ollie said. "It's okay. We're just going to find the key, and then we'll go up one more floor. Right at the top of the stairs, that's where I stay. It's just a room. No dolls. You can sleep on my bed; there's a couch. It's safe. He *promised* me it's safe."

Finally Morgan straightened up and nodded.

Ollie looked around the room. Her skin crawled at the dolls' stiff stares. The light was bad. The room was *packed*. And she couldn't help wondering—*Those dolls. And parts of dolls. Are they people? Were they people? Are they alive? Dead?*

"Let's get started," she whispered.

Morgan nodded again. "Maybe start in the far end? And work our way out?"

"Okay," Ollie said. The only way out of the room was through the door they had come through. If one of the clowns found them, then . . .

We'll hide, that's all, Ollie told herself.

They split up and started going through the room. Their hands and faces glowed red, then blue, with the light outside. Shrieks came through the window. They sounded to her quivering imagination like shrieks of terror. Ollie forced herself to calm down. She moved dolls out of the way as gently as she could. Squinting, touching. Looking for anything in the shape of a key.

She wasn't sure how much time passed. Until Morgan whispered, "Ollie. Ollie! Look."

Morgan was about ten feet away, near the other side of the room. She was staring at a dark corner by the door. She pointed. Ollie followed her finger. Saw it, in a blue flicker from the window. Another doll. It was a man with glasses. Wearing an expression of insane determination. And in one tiny plastic fist, it held a key . . .

"Yes!" Morgan whispered. She crept across the room, around a pile of junk, eyes on the doll.

And then Ollie saw, cold with horror, one of the shadows detach itself from the unmoving ones on the wall. It was crooked, frizzy-haired. She saw it tiptoeing with exaggerated gestures like a cartoon villain, fingers crooked, straight toward Morgan.

"Morgan!" Ollie shouted.

Everything happened quickly. Morgan whipped around. The clown was *right there*, reaching for her. Morgan, with a scream, flung her arm up and threw. Something sparkling flashed through the room, straight toward Ollie. She whipped up an arm, snatched the key out of the air, and shoved it into her jeans pocket. Looked up.

Morgan was gone. She was already gone. The clown,

very tenderly, was sliding a doll into its huge pocket. Then it turned its smile on her, just as the door creaked open and two more clowns clomped into the room. They waved at her. Maybe that was how they did it. Let you see the key, and then they got you . . .

The clowns put their heads together and giggles filled the night, as though they'd played an excellent joke. Then they began doing their cartoon-villain tiptoe toward Ollie.

The door was no good. She went for the window.

She wasn't a climber like Coco, but she'd climbed plenty of trees in her life. She picked up the nearest box of doll parts and hurled it through the window. Then she stepped onto the window frame, glass crunching under her feet, cutting her hands. She reached for the gutter and pulled herself onto the roof.

Her hands were bloody. The light from her bedroom skylight glowed above her. She'd left the window open. Just a quick scramble up the sloping roof and she'd drop into her bedroom. She went for it, heedless of the pain from her cut hands. All she had to do was get there . . .

But there was something wrong. Something different. Something missing.

The giant clown skeleton popped over the roofline. Ollie was barely keeping her grip on the slippery roof tiles; the sight sent her rolling. She caught herself on the gutter. Her heart was hammering like a rabbit's. The clown skeleton was *crawling* over the roof. Its rotted red hair blew in the wind. It turned its empty eye sockets here and there. It didn't have lips. Its grinning red mouth was painted right onto the bones of its skull . . .

It still had teeth.

Ollie heaved herself, panting, back onto the roof. Her hands were slick with bloody sweat. The clown skeleton's empty eye sockets locked on her.

Ollie wondered if touching the skeleton would turn her into a clown too or if it would just flick her off the roof like a bug. It was crouching over her bedroom skylight. Ollie looked down. Clowns were clustered on the ground below the haunted house, grinning up at her. One gave her a thumbs-up. Another was clapping wildly. Two smiling white heads popped out of the broken window.

Give herself even a second to think, and she'd panic. So she ran instead.

Dug in the toes of her sneakers and ran straight up the roof, angling away from the clown skeleton. It swiped at her with a huge hand. She smelled rotten sugar and dust. Her sitting room window was on the attic wall. If she thought about what she was planning even for a second, she'd miss her grip and drop into the dirt and break her legs and then be a doll with broken legs.

But she didn't think. She got to the edge of the roof just ahead of the clown skeleton's fingers. She dropped down and let her feet dangle into space with her agonized hands gripping the gutter. And then she swung her feet inward, through her open sitting room window.

Her hands slipped right off, of course, but she'd managed one swing first. Enough to get her feet into the window and fall on the sitting room floor and not the ground below. She lay there, sobbing for air. Listened for clown feet. Waited for one of them to burst into her room. But nothing happened.

The sound of Morgan's scream still echoed in her ears. The key was heavy in her pocket.

8

BRIAN USUALLY LOVED the drive up from Evansburg to his house at Moose Lodge. The dusty road wound between stands of pine and hemlock. Sometimes you'd get glimpses of meadows between the trees, sloping toward Evansburg, cupped like a marble in the green palm of the mountains.

But Brian wasn't looking at the scenery. His mind ran frantic-fast over everything Tim had said. Need light? Three keys? What did it mean? Was it all some trick of the smiling man's? What should they do?

His mom had to repeat herself, raising her voice from the driver's seat, before he heard her. "Brian—*Brian*, for God's sake, what aren't you kids telling us?"

The phrase *So much, Mom,* almost popped out. "Nothing."

His mom's fingers cramped, visibly, on the wheel. "We

both know that's not true. Why did you insist you needed to talk to Tim Jenkins? Why did you say you aren't safe? Brian, we want you to be safe."

Brian had gotten used to ducking questions, but he didn't think his mom would let him duck this time. Her eyes drilled into his through the rearview mirror. Brian licked his lips. "I can't tell you."

He expected his mom to be furious. He did not expect the hurt expression that crossed her face, nor did he expect his dad to reach across and take his mom's hand in sympathy.

"Honey, why? What have we done to make you not trust us?" Her voice was sad.

If his mom had gotten mad, maybe Brian would have gotten mad right back, like he had by the creek. But her sadness made him feel awful. "I'm trying to keep you safe," he said, his voice going scratchy.

"That's not your job!" his mom retorted. Then she shook her head and went on, quieter. "You've got it wrong. It's my job. And your dad's. So please, son, I'm begging you. Tell me what we need to know to keep you safe. Please. You can talk to us. What's going on with you kids?"

But they were swinging into the driveway of Moose Lodge as she spoke, and Brian was saved from having to answer. A crowd of people—the inn's guests—were standing around outside, looking uneasy. Alarmed. The manager was there too; she was saying, "The police are on their way."

When Brian's parents hurried out of the car, a look of relief spread across the manager's face. Brian was standing plenty near enough to his parents to hear the manager whisper to them, "There's been a break-in."

———

The police looked flummoxed. "Three times today," said one, shaking his head. "Three kids' rooms, nothing taken, so far as anyone can tell. What's going on?"

His partner added, "And all on the same day that Tim Jenkins was found running up the creek. Makes you wonder. Like someone's got a vendetta against kids or something. Maybe keep your doors locked, ma'am. Sir." The cops nodded to Brian and his parents. Then they both drove away.

Brian's parents had to calm down their guests, get the inn settled for the night. His dad started in on it, but his mom, strangely, wasn't helping. She was on the phone, standing out in the yard. Then she put her phone in her pocket, walked through the front door, and said, "That was Roger. He says that the Egg and the Zintners' place were broken into, and Ollie's and Coco's rooms trashed. Just like yours."

Heart pounding, Brian pulled out his phone and saw

about ten missed calls from Coco. He hadn't checked his phone. Too busy staring in horror at his room.

"Brian, *what is going on?*" his mom said.

Brian almost said, *Okay, I don't know if you'll believe me, but here goes . . .*

Then he imagined his mom, who never let suppliers or grumpy guests or black bears in the compost or *anything* stop her, trying to take on the smiling man. Remembered what happened to other people who'd met the smiling man. Remembered scarecrows that had been people. Hollow-eyed ghosts.

"I don't know, Mom."

"Brian, *please.*"

He shook his head and, to his horror, saw tears in her eyes. "Okay, have it your way," she said. "Maybe you think this is a game, or that it doesn't involve anyone but you kids. You're wrong, but think what you like. Apparently Coco told Roger everything. I'll know one way or the other—we're having supper tomorrow, after the parade. But—I wish you'd trust me."

"She *what?*"

His mom just looked at him.

Brian turned away, stumbled upstairs. He started to go to his room, then remembered. Pillows ripped up. His books pulled off the shelves. His favorite hockey stick snapped on the floor. His clothes yanked out of his closet.

He went into the upstairs bathroom instead, shut the door, locked it, and called Coco.

Her voice came breathless over the phone. "Brian—did he—?"

"My room's torn up," Brian said. He kept remembering the splinters of his hockey stick, the crumpled spines of his favorite novels, his mom's face, and wanting to cry. "And you told the grown-ups." His voice was flat.

Coco hesitated. Then she said, "Yes, I did. And my room's ripped up too. And Ollie's. We need to talk about everything. Should we add Phil to the call?"

Brian tried to pull himself together. Getting mad at Coco wouldn't solve anything. "Yeah," he said.

Phil answered on the second ring. They told Phil about their smashed-up bedrooms first.

"My room's okay," Phil said. He sounded a little put out. "I guess the smiling man knows you don't like me as much as you like each other."

Brian's voice echoed on the tile. "You can't possibly be mad that your room *wasn't* messed up."

Phil said, "I— No. But I mean I guess I just—sometimes I get tired of being the less-good Ollie. You know? The not-important friend."

"You're not," Coco said. "Phil, you're not. It's not about getting to Ollie's friends at all. He wanted the watch."

Dead silence.

"The watch?" Phil said.

"Ollie's mom's watch?" Brian said. "That's what they were looking for? Coco, did he—?"

He heard her swallow. "He got it."

"You didn't have it with you?"

"No." Coco's voice was very small. "No, I—I thought— oh, it doesn't matter now, does it? He's got it. Brian, I'm scared."

"You were scared? That's why you went ahead and told the grown-ups? Coco, I get that, but—"

Phil interrupted, "Coco, you told?"

She said, "Yeah. I told my mom and Mr. Adler."

"What did you tell them?" Brian said.

"Everything. The whole story."

Brian let his head fall back, *thump*, against the cool bathroom tile. "Coco—I don't—I get why you did it, but how are we going to keep them safe now?"

"It's not just about being safe. We need help, Brian!" Coco said passionately. "We need help getting Ollie back. We need all the help we can get."

Brian didn't say anything. The bathroom felt hot and airless. *Everything* felt hot and airless, as though their fear had a presence, just like the humid evening. He tried to sound calm. "But what if the smiling man gets your mom? Or Ollie's dad! Or Phil's parents—or mine?"

"What if they could help us end this?" Coco retorted.

"You still should have talked to us first. We're a team. Why didn't you trust us?"

Now she sounded hurt. "You should trust *me*! To make a good decision. Even if it isn't what you'd have done! I'm not *Tiny* anymore. I make good decisions. I beat him once at chess, remember?"

Coco probably didn't mean it, but Brian heard the unspoken part anyway: *While you just sat there, Brian Battersby. You've never beaten the smiling man, never been enough for your friends who needed you . . .*

Brian said nothing.

Phil cut into their silence. He sounded a little pan-icked. "Hey—it would be really something, wouldn't it, if something bad happened while we are all on the phone fighting over something that is already done?"

Phil was right. Brian heard Coco hesitate and then say in a calmer voice, "Right. Okay, so I think—I think that my mom and Mr. Adler believe me."

Brian was skeptical. "Really? Everything?"

Coco amended. "Or at least they believe me enough. We're going to the hospital to try to talk to Tim Jenkins. Tomorrow morning, before the parade. I want to ask him more questions. I wanted to go tonight, but Mom put her foot down."

"My parents and I were supposed to go to the parade,"

Brian said. "But, um, with the weird break-ins, I don't know if they'll—"

Coco said, "We should try and meet at the parade if we can. Ollie's dad is going to call Phil's parents too. He's going to suggest that all of us meet either at my house or at the Egg after the parade tomorrow. To talk about what to do."

Brian was silent, thinking it over.

Coco went on. "At least we'll all be together. We can talk. We can share ideas. We can figure out what to do. I really think the grown-ups can help."

Phil was quiet.

Brian wondered if Coco was trying to convince him or Phil or herself. He thought of the people he loved: his parents, Phil, Coco. Ollie. His friends' families. And he thought of them all under the smiling man's amused gaze.

Then he thought of their families shaking their heads, laughing a little, telling him that what he remembered couldn't possibly be real.

He wondered which it would be.

"Okay," he said. "Parade tomorrow, check. See you there. In the meantime, try and figure out what Tim's clues mean."

Phil said, "What do you guys think it means? It's all confusing."

Coco said, "Three keys. Ghost, mirror, gate. And need light."

Phil asked, "Does light mean we need *light*? Like—flashlights?"

"We can keep lights with us," Brian said. "At all times. Have them, just in case. That's easy. I have headlamps. I'll bring them to the parade tomorrow. I don't know about keys. I mean—house keys, of course, but—"

"There's too much we don't know," Coco said. "I'll see if I can get more from Tim."

"Be careful," Brian said. "And—um, Coco, I'm sorry. I didn't mean to get mad or—act like I didn't trust you. I do. Trust you."

Instantly Coco said, "Same. I trust you guys more than anyone. See you tomorrow."

"Everyone lock their doors," Phil said. "And how does it go? Sleep with one eye open?"

"Yeah," Brian said.

9

OLLIE CLUTCHED THE key so tight that it left a scarlet impression in her palm. She paced the floor, trying to remember everything Morgan had said. Wished she'd had more time to ask questions. Tried not to let that sharp, cut-off scream echo in her head, or imagine empty smiles and unblinking eyes. She splashed water on her face, saw her own eyes red and shadowed in the mirror over the sink.

"Three keys," she said to herself, going back into her bedroom. "This is the first one." She sat on the narrow brass bed and bent to examine the key in the uncertain light of the old-fashioned bedside lamp. The key was about six inches long. It had three jagged teeth on one end. On the other was a tiny, round convex mirror. Ollie could see her face distorted in it. It made her think of the funhouse.

"The first key opens the way to the second key," she said aloud. "The second key opens the way to the third. Third key opens the gate. Find the second key, then the third. Save everyone. All the dolls . . ."

She wished she hadn't said *that* out loud. The dolls weren't something she wanted think about. Not alone, at night. The dolls were everywhere in the carnival. They hung as prizes from every booth. She'd—she'd *shot* at them. Herself. In the archery game. She'd thrown lifesaver-shaped rings at them during the ring toss. Had they been— were they *alive* as dolls? Were they aware? Was that the smiling man's plan for Ollie? When he said stay forever and go wherever you can—did he mean as a *doll*? Because of course, a doll *couldn't* go anywhere. "Oh *God*," said Ollie, and jumped to her feet again. She couldn't keep still. Her brain raced with places that the mirrored key might open. Maybe the funhouse . . . but *where* in the funhouse? The place was huge.

She tried to make plans for the future. She tried not to feel sad. Or despairing. Or betrayed. *Betrayed? Seriously? You knew he was a liar. You knew he was completely untrust-worthy. You* knew, *Ollie.*

Someone tapped on the door of her sitting room. Ollie's head whipped around. What time was it? Late. The midway clown had definitely called midnight, although she wasn't sure about one. She could almost hear her mother's voice: *It's long past your bedtime, Olivia.* The smiling man never knocked this late. Ollie's heartbeat picked up, as though one night outside in the carnival had already given her the habit of fear.

The knock came again.

Ollie shoved the mirrored key far down in the pocket of her hoodie and crept to the sitting room. It was dark except for one of the lamps, turned down low. "Who's there?" she called. It came out a lot shakier than she'd have liked.

Silence. Then she heard a muffled giggle.

She stumbled back into her bedroom. Shut the door, put her back to it. *He said you were safe in the room.*

He's a liar.

She heard another knock. Much louder. From the *bedroom window*. She was sweating with fear. She'd never missed her friends more. She turned her head slowly.

At first she only saw a blur on the other side of the glass, white and red. Then she realized. The clown skeleton was back. Peering in her window. It tapped on the glass with the bones of one finger. It put one empty eye socket to the glass. And then, as she watched, a giant bone arm slipped under the window, where it was open to the summer night, and started groping around. As though it could find her by feel and drag her straight back outside.

Ollie spent the night on the bathroom floor, with the door locked, huddled down small. Listening to the clicking of huge, tireless finger bones in her bedroom. Wondering when the clowns outside her sitting room were going to break in. Wondering what she'd do when they did.

But they didn't break in. The knocking stopped at dawn. Pale summer daylight filtered under the bathroom door. Then Ollie got up and peered back into her bedroom. It was quiet. Empty. She stumbled to bed and collapsed, tear tracks on her face and the key clenched tightly in her sweating fist.

She didn't wake up until late in the day, and that was only because *another* knock came on her door. But this one was accompanied by the smiling man's perfectly ordinary voice calling, "Olivia?"

She blinked bleary eyes. Looked out her window. No clowns in sight. It wasn't dark yet, although it was late afternoon. She made sure the key was still in the pocket of her hoodie. Her hair looked like she'd been dragged backward through a bush, but really, who cared? She'd cleaned her hands as best she could in the sink, but the cuts were aching and stiff. She was pretty sure there was glass in them. She marched to her bedroom door and opened it and found the smiling man sitting at his usual place by the chess table. He'd cleared off the chess pieces and laid out tweezers, alcohol, Band-Aids, and tape.

"Long night?" he said.

She just looked at him.

He leaned back, pressed his fingertips together. "I did say not to leave your room after dark, Olivia."

Ollie crossed her arms, standing in her bedroom doorway. "Were you going to tell me about the dolls?"

"No," he said. "But I assumed you'd be curious eventually and work it out."

"I didn't— You *kidnap* people and—"

A faint smile. "Only the careless, the arrogant, or the unlucky."

"The clowns—they *hunt* . . ."

"Terrible, I know. But you have your pleasant attic. Safe as houses."

"They knocked on my door. They knocked *all night*. The clown skeleton on the roof was *clawing at my window*. Feeling at my floor." Her voice shook.

The smiling man said, "That's your own fault, Olivia. They didn't know you were here, before. Now they do. They will try to get in, I'm afraid. Might be a bit noisy." He looked up at her with a flicker of a smile. "But you're still safe in your rooms. I did promise, didn't I?"

Ollie wondered how long it would take for her safe rooms to feel like a trap. She said, "Why—why any of it? Is it just because you enjoy scaring people? Why couldn't you just leave me and my friends alone? Why can't you just leave everyone alone?"

He narrowed his eyes. "*You* called *me* the last time, didn't you?"

"I didn't have a choice! You got us stuck on a haunted island with a monster! My dad was *dying*."

"For heaven's sake, stop bristling. You are old enough to learn common sense. Sit down, you silly girl, and let me see to your hands."

"Don't you dare," Ollie said. "Don't you dare be nice. You did this to me." She felt like crying again.

"I did not make you climb out a broken window. Now, sit down."

She did, eyes still blurred with tears. She couldn't think what else to do. She didn't want an infection. He got the glass out of her palms. He was quick with the tweezers, businesslike. She wondered where he got Band-Aids, if he just went to Walgreens. Wondering distracted her from the ache in her hands. Washing the cuts out afterward hurt worse, and disinfecting them made her try really hard not to scream. He put on Band-Aids and gathered the wrappers up. "I trust you will refrain from midnight escapades from now on?" he said.

"No promises," said Ollie. She met his eyes. "Do you mean to turn me into a doll?"

"I don't turn people into dolls. The clowns do."

Her stomach cramped.

He said, "If you promise to stay, no one will turn you into a doll." A glimmer of a smile, as though he were reliving a fond memory. "Or a scarecrow. If that's what you're afraid of."

She put her bare feet on the chair, wrapped her arms around her knees. Wondered how long it was until dark. "I don't believe you. You're just planning another trick."

He pursed his lips. "I did say I'd never lie directly to you."

"It doesn't matter. You lie by omission, since you know everything and I know nothing. Friends don't lie to friends *at all*."

An odd expression appeared on his face. He didn't say anything.

Ollie flexed her newly bandaged hands. "I would *never* promise to stay here. I want to go home."

He looked calculating. "I didn't think you were so selfish, Olivia. Or so reckless."

Her face felt hot with anger. "What? Selfish? Reckless? I wouldn't be here at all if I hadn't done everything I could to save *my dad's* life!"

He gave her a patient look. Like she was a small child throwing a tantrum. "And now you're going to risk all your

friends' lives—and their families'—everyone's life, everyone's freedom—just because you're homesick?"

"Me? How? You're the one who's—doing all this!"

He went on remorselessly, "Say your friends come
here. I'll give them their chance, like I promised. And then
what? Your friends will be hunted. They'll be caught.
They'll be hung up in a carnival booth as prizes, for you to
look at, or you'll get yourself caught and will be hanging
up right there with them. So why not save them the terror?
Save yourself the risk? Stay."

She sat perfectly still.

He got up. "I want to show you something."

"I don't want any more rides and lemonade."

"I am not offering you rides and lemonade."

She just looked at him.

He sighed. "Olivia. There is no danger. I promise."

"What, then?"

"I am going to show you what you are risking. That
is all."

He offered a hand. She hesitated a minute more. Then
she scowled and took it. It should have been cold, or
slimy, but it felt just like anyone else's hand. He was so normal in some ways. It made all the rest worse. He opened
the sitting room door with his free hand, pulled her
through it.

Ollie expected the staircase, the dusty landing. Instead she found herself stumbling out onto dry grass. A familiar lawn.

They were standing in front of Coco Zintner's living room window in downtown Evansburg.

The suddenness of it froze her. Ollie stood there, staring, expecting every second to wake up.

But she didn't. With a gasp like a sob, she pressed both hands to the glass. No one inside saw her. She wasn't surprised. The smiling man was right there, and she was sure no one would see her if he didn't want her seen. But she peered in the window like it was a pastry shop and she was starving.

Her dad was there. Coco was there with her mom. Right there inside. Ollie felt tears start to fall. They were having dinner. Her dad smiled and said something. Coco laughed. Coco's mom grinned and got up to get something from the fridge. They looked—they looked just like Ollie and her mom and dad had once. Sitting around the kitchen table. Like a family.

Ollie looked and looked. She didn't know how to feel; shock and longing had built up until they were just a wordless scream inside her. *Dad? Daddy?* She didn't know if she was whispering it or only thinking the words. *Can you see me? Do you want to see me? Do you miss me?*

Dad?

Don't you miss me at all?

But he didn't look up. Just kept on having his dinner. Coco said something. He laughed.

Coco? You guys were supposed to be figuring out how to rescue me.

Don't you want to rescue me?

Suddenly, like the iciest fingers on her heart, it occurred to her that maybe her friends weren't trying. That they weren't looking. That they were happier without her.

"Your father's happy now," said the smiling man. "He missed your mother so much. Every time he looked at you, he had to remember that she was dead." The cicadas on that summer night were louder than his voice, but she heard every word.

"Dad," Ollie whispered to the window. "Dad?"

"He's happy with them," the smiling man went on. "And Coco's happy too—she's always wanted a father. You could ruin their happiness—insist that they try and save you. But will you?"

Ollie didn't say anything.

"Think it over," said the smiling man.

Ollie stared through the window, feeling more and more like a ghost. *I did it for you, Dad,* she thought. *I love you. Don't you care?*

Of course, there was no answer. Finally the living room lights were turned off and the street went dark. Ollie didn't move. She hardly noticed when the smiling man took her hand and opened a door she couldn't see, pushed her back into her sitting room, put another handkerchief in her hand. She hadn't known she was crying. "Tell me what you decide, Olivia," he said, and left her there.

10

COCO'S MOM CALLED her editor at the *Evansburg Independent* the next morning, while Coco took a shower, put on shorts and sneakers, toweled off her hair, and tied it back with a purple scrunchie. The night had been hot. Coco had hardly slept in her sweaty sheets, waking up at every noise.

Still groggy, she started downstairs and stopped six steps from the bottom. Her mom was talking to Mr. Adler in the living room. "My editor's okay with it," she said. "I'll interview hospital staff, do a special piece on how Tim Jenkins appeared at the creek—honestly, why Lethe Creek of all places, he vanished in Rutland—are you sure about this, Roger?"

Coco stood there, listening. Their voices came clearly to the stairwell.

"Sure of what?" asked Ollie's dad.

"Encouraging whatever's going on with Coco."

"We asked her to tell us, and she told us. How do we expect her to decide to trust us if we don't trust her?"

Exactly, thought Coco. *Thanks, Mr. Adler.*

Her mom sounded frustrated. "Roger—I don't—I'm not sure I like it. Encouraging her. I get what you're saying about trust, but she's imagined all this. She needs to know what's real and what's not."

Coco felt like she'd been kicked.

"There's something real in all this," insisted Ollie's dad. "Has to be. Someone broke into our houses, Zelda. Yours and mine and the Battersbys'. Coco *knew* that whoever it was in the Egg had come here. She knows *something* real."

"Yes," said her mom, voice high with tension. "And whoever it was, it wasn't some supernatural monster! Roger, don't make this about you."

"What do you mean, about me?" he asked.

"I mean—" Coco could hear her mom taking a deep breath. "I mean, Coco says your daughter isn't dead. And you want to believe that."

Mr. Adler's voice turned frankly disbelieving. "And so you think that I'm delusional?"

"Hopeful," said her mom. "Roger, please, don't be angry. I'm just trying to do what's best for Coco, that's all."

"So am I," he said.

"She's not yours!" her mother snapped. Coco covered her mouth silently. *But I could be, Mom,* she thought. *Why are you saying this?* She wanted Mr. Adler to argue. Wanted him to say, *I know she's yours, Zelda, but I love her. She could be my daughter, and I could be her dad.*

But he didn't. He didn't defend Coco or himself or anything. Her stomach felt hollow with hurt. Mr. Adler just said, his voice tired, "You're right, of course, Zelda. She's yours. Do you still want us to come with you to the hospital?"

"Yes, definitely," said her mom, in a softer voice. "I don't want to fight. We'll bring some flowers from the yard. I promised Coco. Where is she?"

Coco stomped down the stairs, hoping neither of them noticed that she'd had to wipe tears off her face. "Ready to go?" she said. She couldn't look at either of them. She'd have said something babyish, like *You don't believe me, Mom, and Mr. Adler doesn't want me, so why am I even trying?*

She knew it wasn't true. But she couldn't help thinking it as they all got in the car and drove away.

———

The hospital was in an old, sprawling building. The pride of Evansburg. It had been a mental hospital once. Coco had learned that in school. The biggest one in the state. But that was a long time ago. Now it was a modern hospital, with three floors. The only reminder of its past was the age-dark brick on the outside and the oddly small windows.

Ordinarily Evansburg hospital was a sleepy place. But that day it was mobbed. There were news trucks everywhere. Reporters were camped in the front lobby, typing furiously on their phones, watching everyone who went in and out.

Coco had collected a get-well gift of phlox and sunflowers from the garden. Her sweaty hand clenched around the flowers.

All three of them went to the front desk. Coco was wondering if they had a chance at being let in, since all those important-looking journalists were being kept waiting in the lobby. But Ollie's dad said, smiling, "Doris, how's the foot?" to the receptionist. They knew each other. Most people in Evansburg knew each other.

"Roger Adler, as I live and breathe!" Doris said. "And Zelda Zintner! Did Jeffrey send you?" Jeffrey was the editor of the *Evansburg Independent*. "And you must be Coco. How are you, dear?"

"I'm fine, thank you, ma'am," Coco said. Maybe if she was extra polite, they'd get in. "How are you?"

"Oh, I'm just dandy. All three of you were there when that poor boy was found, weren't you?"

Not for the first time, Coco, who only moved to Evansburg a year ago, wondered how news got around.

"Yes, at the swimming hole," Coco's mom said. "Listen, Doris, I know you're not allowing visitors—just as well, or you'd have a mob upstairs—but I have an assignment from Jeff to cover this for the *Independent*, and Coco brought flowers for Tim Jenkins. She was the first one to spot him, actually. Think we could go up?"

Doris frowned at all the reporters in the lobby. "Well, I'm supposed to be keeping people out, Zelda."

Coco's heart sank.

Doris went on, "But I'd hate to have these folks get the scoop over our local paper. I'm sure you'll do it kindly, not harass that poor family. They've had a terrible time. Ruth is still missing, and they're desperate to hear what Tim has to say. Look, you slip on through that door. Room 308, and if anyone asks, I don't know a thing about it."

Coco's heart lightened. They'd done it! "Sure thing," Mr. Adler said. "Thanks, Doris."

They got in the elevator. It was big enough for people on gurneys, with a large mirror on the back wall. The elevator dinged, and the doors closed. "Huh," her mom said. "I didn't press a button." She pressed the button for the third floor, but no button lit up. "Weird," she said. "Well, I hope we get the right floor. And while we're hoping things,

I hope they get Tim to talk soon. I know he's had an awful time. But poor little Ruth."

Coco frowned at the blank row of elevator buttons. The elevator was slowing down. The doors slid open. "Let's see—what floor did we wind up on?" said her mom. "I don't recognize this."

The hallway was narrow, and a bit dim. And it was also quiet. Empty.

Mr. Adler said, "Must be a part of the hospital they never renovated. I didn't know the elevator even went to this floor." He pushed the button for the third floor. The elevator doors didn't close.

The mirror at the back of the elevator reflected the dim hallway. In the mirror, the hallway looked even darker. Coco's palms had gone clammy. Mr. Adler quit mashing the elevator buttons. It wasn't doing any good.

"Well," he said. "Guess we'll just need to find the stairs."

Coco pushed the button herself. Nothing. Even pushed the emergency button. Silence.

"It's okay, Coco," her mom said. "It's not an emergency. We'll just go find some stairs."

"I don't like this," Coco said.

"A bit sinister, no?" Mr. Adler said cheerfully. "But it's just a malfunctioning elevator. We'll stick together. It's okay."

"This is the kind of thing he does," Coco said. "The smiling man." It felt weird to say *the smiling man* to the adults. *Smiling man* sounded like a childish superstition, not a real menace. She forged on. "He makes the world go wrong and sideways, and *creepy*."

She saw her mom and Mr. Adler exchanging puzzled glances. She wondered how much of her story they'd *really* believed. But Mr. Adler said, "Okay, Coco. Do you think we *shouldn't* go look for stairs?"

She didn't know what else to do. "I think we have to," she said reluctantly. "But we need to keep together. And—and be careful of mirrors."

Her mom gave Coco a doubtful look. Like she wanted to say, *That's just superstition, Coco.* But she didn't.

Coco was still holding her flowers, so her mom held her by the wrist. Mr. Adler took her other hand, and they started to walk down the hall. The hall was completely quiet, except for the shush of their footsteps. Small barred doors studded the walls on either side. "Incredible," Mr. Adler said. "I honestly thought there wasn't anything of the old hospital left."

That didn't make Coco feel any better. "Where are the stairs?"

"Don't know," Mr. Adler said. "But there'll be an exit sign. Required by law, you know."

Coco didn't see an exit sign. Suddenly there was a

loud, echoing *clang*, like someone had slammed a metal door somewhere ahead. They all jumped. "Hello?" Coco's mom called. "Hello—is someone there? We managed to get off on the wrong floor, and—" There was another clang. Coco felt the sweat slicking her palms now. The corridor dead-ended. They had to turn left or right. The hallways looked identical. No exit signs. Dim lights in the ceiling, little pools of shadow where the light didn't touch.

Another clang. This one at their backs. They turned around. No one was there. Coco saw the grown-ups looking uneasy now. *Clang*, from the leftmost corridor. But before they could turn to look, a crash from the right. As though people were banging on metal doors somewhere out of sight.

The clangs came faster and faster. Run? But where? Was it even dangerous? Where were the stairs? "Stop it!" Coco's mom shouted, looking strangely fragile in the storm of noise.

The clanging stopped. They all looked around wildly. "Hello?" a voice said—a normal voice. Rapid footsteps sounded on the linoleum. "You people lost?"

It was a guy in a uniform. Coco recognized him. Officer Fier, from the swimming hole. "Oh, thank goodness," Coco's mom said. "Must have been a raccoon in the ductwork or something—scared us half to death. Can you point us to the stairs, please? Elevator isn't working."

"Certainly. Right this way," Officer Fier said.

The two grown-ups started off. But Coco stood rooted to the spot. Then Officer Fier glanced back over his shoulder and smiled at her. And Coco was sure.

She caught up and hissed at him, "Where's Ollie?"

"My dear, is that any way to greet an old friend?" He looked like he was enjoying himself.

"No, it isn't," Coco said. "Good thing we aren't friends. You promised us a chance to get Ollie back. I want our chance. Tell me what I need to know. Where's Ollie?"

He gave her a measuring look. "You really want to know?"

She met his eyes. "Yes."

He said, "Have you thought what it might cost—trying to get Ollie back? Have you thought whom you might—endanger?"

Coco didn't answer. She tried to look strong and stubborn. But she couldn't help her eyes sliding sideways, to where her mom and Ollie's dad were walking ahead of them down the creepy hallway, oblivious to the conversation. "Exactly," the smiling man said. "Now, if you were to promise to give up your quest to find your friend, you'd never hear from me again. You won't even remember you had a friend named Olivia Adler. Won't that be comforting? What you don't know can't hurt you."

The air in the hallway seemed to be getting colder. "And if I say no?" Coco said.

"You'll fail. And I'll have you all." He wasn't smiling at all, right then. "I'll gather you up one by one. You and Brian and Phil. Your parents. Everyone. And the world will just forget you. You know it will. I can do that. Could you live with yourself if something happened to your mother? To Ollie's dad? He could be your dad, you know, someday. And you won't have to do a thing. Just *stop trying*."

How long was this corridor? The grown-ups strode ahead, completely unaware. Coco heard someone laughing wildly behind one of the barred doors. Then the laughter turned to sobs. She didn't turn to look. He was just trying to scare her. He liked to scare people. Coco's voice was small, but she said, "I beat you once. I can do it again."

"Not this time."

"I won't abandon Ollie," Coco said. "I promised, she's my friend, I *can't*." But she knew he could hear the anguish in her voice. "Leave our families alone!"

"I told you to leave *me* alone. If you do, I'll return the courtesy."

"You should have left us alone first!"

"That is not what we are discussing."

Now someone *screamed* from behind one of the metal doors. Coco lurched sideways. The smiling man caught her elbow. Coco wrenched away from him. "Where are we?" The grown-ups walking ahead still didn't turn. They were like zombies, Coco thought. Walking, unthinking. *He made them like that. He does whatever he wants, it's fun for him, he doesn't care.*

"The world is full of ghastly corners," he said. "I like ghastly corners. Hospitals often have one. This one is special. People who were locked up in life make excellent ghosts." He gave the hallway a look of approval. "Now, your answer?".

She took a deep breath. "No."

He stopped walking.

"Save me from stubborn girls," he muttered. "All right, how about this? If you want to be with Olivia so much, come with me now. I'll take you straight to her. You both promise to stay. Everyone else forgets you. Everyone else is happy."

Coco's head spun. What was best for Ollie? Her parents? Brian and Phil? *Herself*? "Why?" she demanded. "Why any of it? Why are you making us do this?"

"I enjoy it," said the smiling man. "Now, I am curious. Your answer?"

Coco screwed up all her courage. There was, in the end, only one answer. "You promised a chance. I want our chance. Where's Ollie?"

He smiled. It wasn't one of his nicer smiles. "So be it. Tim Jenkins told you all you need to know. Come at night. I'll be waiting."

"Start your game," Coco said, trying to sound braver than she felt. "We're ready."

"Oh," he said gently, "it's already begun."

And then Coco blinked and saw the exit sign. Officer Luke Fier had caught up with her mom and Mr. Adler. "Here you go," he said. "Right down there." He turned back to Coco. "Are you all right?" he asked her with cheerful concern. "A little hot in here, isn't it? Well, how about I give the poor boy your flowers, and *you* go out and enjoy the parade? I'm so sorry you all got lost."

Both Mr. Adler and her mother were smiling at him warmly. "Thank you so much," her mom said. "You're right—I can't imagine what I was thinking, planning to disturb that poor boy. We'll go straight out."

"Mom?" Coco whispered.

But her mom was already going down the stairs.

"Coco, are you okay?" asked Mr. Adler.

"Are we going to interview Tim?" she asked, hearing her voice shake.

Mr. Adler frowned. "Tim? Oh—no. I mean, what's the point now? Officer Fier will deliver your flowers."

Officer Fier was just disappearing down the stairs ahead of them, with Coco's flowers in his hand. He turned back and gave her a wink. He was whistling.

11

WHEN BRIAN SAW Coco standing with her mom and Mr. Adler amid the milling crowd, waiting for the parade to start, he knew something was wrong. Oh, she was trying to look okay. But she held herself too still and jumped at every sudden noise.

He hurried up to her. "Coco, what—"

"I saw the smiling man," Coco whispered. "He was at the hospital. He tried to make me give up, say we weren't going to try and save Ollie!"

"What did you tell him?"

"No, of course. But he says if we do it, he'll get all our families too . . ." She broke off, shivering. "And maybe he can. It was so easy for him to make Mom and Mr. Adler act weird. And it seemed like he was enjoying himself."

"Okay," Brian said, suppressing a shiver of his own,

trying to think what to do. His heart beat double time; he scanned the crowd. "We need to talk to Phil. Let's go get him and then you can tell us everything, all right?"

"Yeah," Coco said. She shivered again, despite the heat. Main Street was packed. Almost everyone in Evansburg was there. It was organized chaos. The high school cheerleaders were getting ready to join the parade. The town green was milling with local cows. They were going to parade too.

"Hi, kids! Hi, everyone!" said Mr. Easton, their homeroom teacher. He looked a little odd in shorts. Brian had only ever seen him in khaki pants and a flannel shirt. His mustache was neatly brushed. "Another scorcher, eh?" He whipped out a handkerchief and wiped his face. The grownups were talking about something related to the paper, and the school board.

"Phil's with Mikey over by the cows—Mikey wanted to pet them," Brian said. "Let's go."

"You guys planning on taking off?" Brian's dad asked, seeing them with their heads together.

"Just to the cows." Coco's voice was thin.

"Over there," added Brian. "On the town green. You'll literally be able to see us."

Brian's parents looked at each other. Finally, Brian's mom said, "Okay, but your word—you *promise*—that you won't go anywhere else."

Brian and Coco nodded, and eeled away through the crowd. Greetings volleyed in from all sides, mostly at Brian, whose sense of humor and hockey-star status made him very popular. He kept close to Coco.

"Tell me," Brian said, while they were walking.

Coco did, in a rush, stumbling over her words.

"Good for you," Brian said, when she was done. "You did the right thing. Told him right where he can put his pathetic *offers*."

"I guess," Coco said. She still looked unhappy. She wrapped her arms around herself. "But I— Brian, I didn't manage to get anything more from Tim Jenkins. They wouldn't let me talk to him. It was like the smiling man changed their minds about it. *Poof.* All I know is what Tim told us first. About the light and the keys and stuff."

They got to the town green, where fifteen or so heifers were waiting to walk in the parade. Phil waved. He had his little brother by the hand. Mikey was reaching up to pat the white-spotted nose of a cow.

"Phil," Brian said, low. "Coco saw the smiling man."

Phil went pale. "Geez," he said. "Where?"

"Phil, I'm hungry," Mikey interrupted.

"Well, that's cool, do I look like I'm made of snacks?" Phil demanded, sounding tense.

Mikey's lip quivered.

Phil bent hastily to him. "No, wait, sorry. Look, Mikey,

we're all going to go climb that tree to watch the parade and keep an eye on things. Sound like fun?"

"Yeah!" Mikey cried at once. "Let's climb the tree!"

"You can only come with us if you're not a loud little cookie monster," Phil said.

Mikey mimed zipping his lips and throwing away the key.

Phil turned to Brian and Coco. "At least we'll be able to see what's going on from the tree. And we'll be alone, and we can decide what to do. Mikey won't know what we're talking about. I told Mom I'd keep a close eye on him." Phil might complain about Mikey, but he loved his little brother.

"No, it's a good idea," Brian said. "At least it will be shady up there."

"Yeah," Coco said. "I wish it would rain."

They all glanced up. But the sky was the same hard dusty blue it had been for most of the summer.

The tree was a massive old sugar maple in the middle of the town green. Coco climbed up first, and then Brian. Phil handed Mikey up to him, and Brian settled him on a wide, sturdy limb, not too far off the ground. "Don't *wiggle*, 'kay?" Brian told him.

Mikey just nodded, swinging his feet. His eyes were still on the cows. People were collecting on the green, calling to each other, laughing. The whole town was there.

Phil climbed up last. They all settled in.

"Okay," Brian said. "Coco, you first. Tell Phil what happened at the hospital."

Coco told Phil what she'd just told Brian.

"It's already begun?" Phil said. "What does that mean?" Goose bumps rose on his arms, despite the heat.

"Let's not think about that," Brian said firmly. "Let's go over what we know."

Phil nodded. He looked shaky. "Tim got kidnapped at the carnival in Rutland. Along with Ruth," he offered.

"Is it the same carnival that's coming here?" put in Coco. "With the county fair?"

Both boys nodded. "Every year," Brian said. "There's the fair, there's the demolition derby—" He paused. He loved the demolition derby. The cars made such a fantastic *smash*.

Coco said, *"Ahem?"*

"And the carnival," Brian finished hastily. "Carnivals travel all over. Not just Vermont. All over the country."

"Okay. And we think the smiling man got Tim and Ruth Jenkins at this carnival," Coco said. "The same carnival that's coming here."

"Is that where we have to go? To get Ollie back? The carnival?" Phil asked.

They all thought about it. "Seems pretty likely," Brian

said. He added, "Tim said *needs light* and *keys*. I dunno what *keys* means, but I have headlamps with me. In case he meant *light* literally."

Brian dug into his backpack and handed one headlamp to Coco and one to Phil. They each tucked them in their pockets.

"So what next?" Phil asked.

Brian wasn't sure. Coco opened her mouth to say something, but a roar of noise interrupted her. The parade was starting. They all swiveled to look. First there was the mayor and the town select board—Mr. Wilson and a couple of their neighbors—marching past their perch. Then the high school cheerleaders, waving pom-poms. Then a few parade floats.

And then came the cows. Mikey went round-eyed with delight. The cows strolled down Main Street, accompanied by a strong smell of hot cowhide. Large green cowpats speckled the street behind them.

Brian heard cheering and some old-fashioned, tooting music.

Coco grabbed Brian's arm. Floating between the branches of the maple was a—head. A grinning, milk-white, red-mouthed head. It was huge. It had curling red hair and garish pink cheeks and a big delighted smile. It had a fluffy collar around its neck, but no body.

Just the floating, grinning white head.

"It's a balloon," whispered Phil.

Neither Coco nor Brian said anything. Under the balloon was a parade float, the biggest one of all, emitting that blaring music.

The people on the float were kind of colorless. They had frizzy hair and shapeless clothes. They reached into their pockets and threw out candies. They waved at the crowd.

"Those guys are kind of weird-looking, aren't they?" Phil commented.

"Hey, look," Coco said. Her voice was tight with strain. "There are more of those guys in the crowd. With the frizzy hair. Throwing candies. Does it seem like they're kind of—looking for something—to you?"

Above them, the giant clown-head balloon bobbed and grinned.

Brian could see what Coco was saying. The people on the float were staring fixedly at the crowd, their heads turning here and there. As though they really were looking for something. Or someone . . .

"Could that float have anything to do with the smiling man?" Coco whispered. "Could those guys be looking for us? Why, though? He found me in the hospital just fine."

"Dunno. But I'm pretty sure they can't see us," Brian said. "We're behind the branches. Glad we climbed a tree."

The cows were shaking their heads back and forth, as though troubled by flies. Someone below the tree picked up a candy. Then another person. "Mikey!" yelled Phil suddenly. Mikey had scrambled down from his perch below them in the maple tree and was grabbing at candies himself. "Mikey, get back up here!"

But Mikey had never listened to anyone—certainly not them—once in his life. He had a handful of chocolates in his fist, and instead of climbing back up, he sprinted away through the crowd in search of more. "Mikey!" Phil bellowed. He scrambled down the tree. "Get back here, you'll get stepped on!"

But Mikey had already vanished.

Brian and Coco hesitated. Then they scrambled down in Phil's wake. Came out into the sun of the town green. Everything seemed to happen in slow motion. Brian saw a sea of faces and, beyond that, the weird guys on the carnival float, the clown balloon bobbing overhead.

Then Brian glimpsed a familiar face. Just for a second. A man with fair-ish hair, and pale-ish eyes. He winked at Brian. Vanished into the crowd.

And then, suddenly, all the cows in the parade went mad. Eyes wild, foam flying from their wide-open mouths. Brian saw Phil Greenblatt grab his brother and yank him out of the way of a maddened heifer. They both fell, rolling in a crumpled heap. Brian and Coco ran, shoving to help.

As they did, the strangers on the float stopped throwing chocolate. Their eyes locked on the three kids. Brian could almost feel their stares, like a clammy cold thing on his skin. His first thought was, *If they were looking for us, they found us.*

His second thought was, *They look a little like dogs that have seen a rabbit.*

Right as the thought crossed his mind, every person on the float broke into a wide smile.

12

OLLIE HAD PLAYED chess with the smiling man six times since the night she saw her dad, but the smiling man hadn't mentioned it. Maybe he was giving her time to think. Or maybe he was waiting for something to happen. What, she didn't know, and that made her nervous.

While the train clacked down its track, Ollie turned the first key over in her hand, and thought. Then the train stopped again, and the carnival unfurled like a poisonous flower in the summer dust. As soon as it did, Ollie went straight to the funhouse, with the mirrored key tucked snug in her jeans pocket.

Of course, it wasn't her first visit to the funhouse. But she'd never searched it over as carefully as she did now. She tapped every mirror, trying to find hidden passages behind them. She looked everywhere for a keyhole. She tried waving the key in front of the mirrors to see if a key-hole would magically appear.

But nothing happened. The funhouse remained just as it always had. Galleries and corridors of mirrors, kids squealing and making faces in the glass. Laughter echoing. Stairs, ramps, spirals, narrow passages, all twisting your face into a stranger's. Carnival music drifting in through the walls. Ollie had the first key. But she couldn't find any clue about the second.

Her frustration mounted.

The second night of that stop, two lost kids appeared in front of the haunted house window. It was after dark. Ollie saw them down there and remembered what Morgan had said about kids getting lost. That sometimes the clowns found them.

And these kids certainly looked lost.

She didn't know what she could do, but she ran downstairs anyway. To her shock, they could see her. *Probably,* she thought, *getting lost means you stumbled behind the mist somehow, where I am. Where the clowns are.*

She tried to warn them.

She was too late.

But the kids told her two things she hadn't known.

That night, she sat upright in her bed, shivering, trying not to remember how Ruth Jenkins had screamed. Trying to focus on facts.

The kids said we're in Rutland. I'm pretty sure the next stop is Evansburg.

Maybe Brian and Coco and Phil will come soon. Maybe they'll help me.

Maybe they aren't coming.

Or maybe they'll come and be turned to dolls.

The next time the smiling man came to play chess, he said, "Will you stay, Olivia?"

She took a deep breath. She looked him straight in the face. "My friends are coming. And I'm going home with them."

She didn't say anything else. She moved a piece.

A *click* made her look up. He was gone. He'd resigned the game. The *click* was the black king toppling over.

Well, Ollie thought, *I really,* really *need the second key now.* She couldn't think where it would be besides the funhouse. But she'd only gone into the funhouse by day.

Maybe she'd always known that she'd have to go in by night. She'd found the first key at night, after all. She imagined all the lights going out. Or hearing invisible, clacking footsteps. Or giggles at her back. Or seeing a clown in the mirror ahead of her, clowns in the mirrors on all sides, closing in.

A tiny part of her wondered if it wouldn't have been easier to tell the smiling man, *Yes, I'll stay,* and go on down the road. She was used to the train. She wouldn't *die* on the train, or be turned into something horrible. He'd promised.

No, she thought. *No.* It wasn't just about her. It was every single person stuck in that carnival. If she had any chance of saving them—she had to try.

So one August morning, Ollie got up, thinking hard. There was a chance she wasn't coming back to those rooms. Either the funhouse would get her, or she'd get the next key. There was even a chance Brian and Coco would find her rooms if they made it into the carnival to look for her. Ollie wanted to leave them a message. She wanted to leave something behind. Even if it was the longest long shot in the world, she didn't want to just disappear into the funhouse at night without a word to anyone.

But how? It wasn't like there was a pen or paper lying around.

Frowning, Ollie went to her bookcase. Looked at the books. Started to smile. Pulled out *Alice's Adventures in Wonderland.*

After she'd left her message, Ollie went out and walked around the carnival. She just wanted a few hours in the sun. She got a lemonade and a funnel cake. Maybe the sugar would keep her alert. But she found that she could hardly swallow; the sugar curdled in her stomach.

She wished she had a flashlight.

Day turned to dusk and found Ollie standing in the shadow of the funhouse. She planned to go in before the carnies turned to clowns. Maybe they wouldn't spot her. Maybe it would all be okay. But when she raised the last of her lemonade to her mouth, the drink sloshed, and Ollie realized that her hands were shaking.

Then she saw that there was a spot of stillness in the happy crowd on the midway. One person who wasn't moving.

She gave the smiling man a defiant look. Took a big bite of funnel cake. It made a solid lump in her throat. He said, "Don't, Olivia. There's nothing in there that you can find."

She drank her lemonade. Coughed. "No? What am I supposed to do, then? Stay in my room and listen to your *clowns* knocking all night? I think the key's in here. I'm playing to win. I'll take my chances."

"Not in there." His glance flicked up the soaring funhouse, its mirrored sides beautiful with the colors of the carnival lights. "You won't have a chance in there." He hesitated, and then he said, "No one has a chance in there. Not at night. There's no way out."

"I'm still going." Ollie wished her voice sounded stronger. "Unless you have a better suggestion. You could be lying by omission again."

He was silent. He looked angry. From his perspective, he'd probably tried everything to get her to stay, Ollie thought. Chess. Funnel cake. Being nice. Scaring her. Threatening her family.

He must really want me to stay.

He wouldn't be trying so hard, would he, if he didn't think I had a chance to escape.

The thought flowed into her like hot chocolate, soothing her fear. "You could come in with me," Ollie said, only half joking. "If you're so worried."

"I don't protect people from their own stupidity," he snapped, and now he did look angry. Also uncertain, which was unlike him.

"Okay, well, I'm going in before your clowns see me. But I have one question. Just one. I think it's the last question I'll ever ask you, so I kind of hope you'll answer." She wished he wouldn't look angry and uncertain. It made him look too human.

"Ask," he bit off.

"Why?" Ollie said. "Why do you do this?"

He didn't joke, or say something condescending. He didn't pretend to misunderstand or to not hear her at all. Something changed in his face, though. It grew—stranger, somehow. Remote. He spoke slowly, as though weighing out each word before letting it fall. "Once, a long time ago, it was easy to find yourself—elsewhere. The world was—oh, what's the word? You say *uncanny* in English, I suppose. From the Scots, sixteenth century: *unknowable*. The world was uncanny. It was full of strange things. Strange people. Strange worlds. Ways behind the mist. People *believed* the world was uncanny, and their very conviction kept the ways open."

Ollie listened, silent.

"There are fewer ways now," said the smiling man. "But some remain. The places where the world turns frightening, strange, sideways. And that is where you will find me. Tricking people through the mist. That is my— job, if you like. To keep the way between worlds open."

Ollie stared. "But you—so you *have* to do all this?"

A very faint smile. "That was another question, Olivia. But all right. Sometimes, not always."

"You can't just let me go home, can you?"

He shook his head.

"Okay," Ollie said, and turned her back on him. If she hesitated, her courage would fail her, so she didn't hesitate. She went inside with the last of the daylight and shut the door behind her.

It was the day of the parade in Evansburg. But Olivia Adler didn't know that. The smiling man watched her go, frowning. But she didn't know that either.

13

THEY ALL CONVENED late that evening at the Egg. It wasn't dark yet, but the sun was dipping. Brian kept checking his pocket to make sure his headlamp was there, like the little light by itself could keep the darkness back. Coco and her mom and Mr. Adler were already back at the Egg when Brian and his parents showed up. Mr. Adler was slicing bread. "I thought sandwiches, honestly," he said. "It's so hot, who wants to turn on the oven?"

"Thanks for hosting, Roger," Brian's mom said. "I'm so glad we're going to be talking. Shame about the parade. Those cows."

"Do you think the Greenblatts will make it?" Coco's mom asked. "Have you heard anything from the hospital?"

Brian's mom had been talking to Phil's mom. "Mikey's going to be all right. Cast for him and crutches for Phil, but it could have been worse."

Brian glanced at the sky, saw Coco doing the same. It was nearly full dark. He wished the hospital had been faster.

The Greenblatts showed up just as the last of the light trickled from the sky. Mikey was a bit loopy with painkillers. His arm was in a lime-green cast. Phil's ankle was wrapped in an Ace bandage, and he hopped on crutches. He looked frustrated and a little scared. "A lot of use I'm going to be," he muttered to Brian and Coco. "I was already the less-good Ollie, and I can't even walk now."

"Phil, don't say that," Coco said. "You're not. We don't even know what's going to happen."

Phil just shook his head and gave his ankle a dark look.

"Hope you're hungry," Mr. Adler was saying. "No, have a seat, Zelda. I've got this. I have all the fixings. Taking sandwich orders now. Ham and Swiss? Peanut butter and jelly? Peanut butter, bacon, and pickle? Something stranger? I love a challenge, and I cater to all tastes. Here, Coco, could you go into the pantry and get a few bags of chips? Brian, do you mind going and seeing what we have for drinks? There's root beer, I know. Pink lemonade. The grown-ups can grab their own—"

He got them sitting around the living room with loaded paper plates on their knees. The mood in the room improved. It felt like a dinner party. But Brian kept looking at the doors. The windows. He saw Phil and Coco doing the same. He remembered seeing the smiling man there in the crowd. He remembered how the strangers on the float had smiled. He wished he knew what was going to happen.

"Okay," Brian's mom said. She put her paper plate aside. They all sat up straighter. "Roger, you said the kids wanted to tell us all something. Is now a good time?"

Instead of answering directly, Mr. Adler looked at Brian, Coco, and Phil. "You have the floor, for whatever you want to tell us." And then Mr. Adler fixed his dark eyes—just like Ollie's eyes—on all their parents. "And we, the adults, promise not to say anything until you're done."

The grown-ups all nodded.

Brian got up. It was just his family there. And his best friends' families. But he still felt vulnerable. He went over the beats of the story in his head, and it sounded— ridiculous. Unbelievable. Like a book he'd have read, not something that might have *happened* to them. "Here goes. But look"—he stared directly at his parents—"this is the story. No matter how wild it sounds, I *promise* you, by— whatever you want me to swear by. That it's true."

Glances were exchanged. His parents nodded encouragingly.

Brian started talking. No one said anything. When he got tired, Coco got up and took over. She looked a bit nervous, but her voice didn't squeak once. Brian tried not to watch the ring of intently listening faces. Tried not to think how absurd it all sounded. Ghosts? Evil scarecrows? How could his parents possibly believe all this? They were going to be kind and patient and put him straight into therapy. Which might be helpful, except he didn't see the therapist believing it had all happened either.

Coco stopped speaking. They'd gotten to the end. Coco had finished the story with the parade that day—the music, the float. The cows losing their minds.

It was completely dark outside.

The tension in the room felt like a string about to snap. For a few minutes, no one said anything.

Then Brian's dad said, "Let me get this straight. For almost a whole year—ever since last October—there's been a shady character *harassing* you?"

"Um," Brian said. It wasn't exactly how he'd have put it, but . . . "Um, yeah."

His dad looked outraged. "And you didn't tell us? Brian, this is what parents are *for*. This lowlife isn't coming near you again. Where is he? I don't care what he calls himself. He's going straight to jail for harassment. Assault. *Kidnapping*. You think he has Ruth Jenkins? And *Ollie*? We're calling the police. We're going to get to the bottom of this right now." Brian had never seen his dad so worked up.

"Brian, I'm glad you told us," his mom said. "We'll take care of you."

Brian exchanged astonished looks with Coco and Phil. He had imagined his parents disbelieving, amused, even scared. Oddly enough, he had never imagined protective fury. For about a minute, he basked in it. It felt like being wrapped in a warm blanket on a cold day. Like being a little kid again. *They'll take care of us.*

Mr. Greenblatt said, "Calling himself Luke Fier, you say? Officer Fier?" He was making notes intently on his phone. Mr. Greenblatt was a lawyer. "We can start by filing a complaint. The police can get a warrant to search his residence. Might be tricky since he's on the force—and he was involved in the kidnapping last October? And has something to do with the carnival where those kids . . . ? Man, this slimeball gets around. You should have told us sooner."

The grown-ups' phones were coming out. They were googling, making notes. Their heads were together. Busily solving the problem. Could it really be that simple?

But one by one, all their parents looked up. "I lost the signal," said Mrs. Greenblatt, just as Coco's mom said, "The Wi-Fi isn't working."

Phil jerked upright and winced as he accidentally put weight on his bad ankle. Brian and Coco exchanged glances. Brian looked at the lamp beside the couch. Coco was peering through the window into the dark yard. "Honey?" Coco's mom said.

"Brian?" his dad said.

Brian said, "You lose—signal. Connectivity. Whatever. When he's close. Or his—his people. Supernatural stuff. And then, when they're *closer*, the lights flicker . . ."

As though his voice had made it happen, the overhead lights wavered. The adults exchanged looks of anxious confusion. Brian realized, with a sinking heart, that their parents had heard their story and pulled out the concrete stuff. Words they knew. Like *bad man, kidnapping, danger*. But their parents had imagined a single lunatic, dangerous to children. A danger that they could erase with their sheer grown-up presence. They hadn't taken the stuff about monsters literally.

Mikey, still on his mother's lap, suddenly woke up. "Mom!" he gasped, wide-eyed. "Mommy! I—I dreamed I couldn't move! And you were gone—"

Mrs. Greenblatt shushed him. "Hush, baby. It's okay. It was just a dream."

The lights dipped again. Brian felt his heart sink. He had hoped, for a few minutes, that the grown-ups would take the fear and the danger and make it into something simple. Manageable. Like banishing a bogeyman from under a five-year-old's bed.

But their parents looked as awkward and uncertain as he and Coco had last October, when their school bus broke down and they found themselves first pulled into the smiling man's world.

Coco was still looking outside. "There's someone on the lawn," she breathed.

"Probably just someone out for an evening walk," said Mr. Adler. But he was staring out the windows in the same direction as Coco. His shoulders were tense.

Brian crossed to Coco, who was standing by Phil's chair. The three put their heads together. "What did you see?" Brian whispered.

"Just a shadow," Coco said, her face pale and anxious. "Sort of like the one I saw yesterday. Right before someone broke into the house."

"Could they get in again?" Phil asked. His eyes were on his wrapped ankle.

"But what is it?" Brian said. "It can't be scarecrows this time, can it?"

They exchanged uneasy looks.

Phil said, "We need to get to the carnival, right? Can't we sneak out? Better to run than to stay put, anyway. Maybe the grown-ups could drive?"

"Will the cars even work?" Coco muttered.

Neither of the boys answered. None of them would bet on it.

The lights dimmed again.

Brian was reaching for his headlamp just as the lights went out entirely. He, Coco, and Phil turned on their headlamps simultaneously. The room filled with a ghostly white glow.

But just as quick, Mr. Adler said sharply, "Turn them off. Right now."

Startled, they obeyed. Mrs. Greenblatt was still trying to soothe Mikey. Brian's parents and Phil's dad had turned on their phone lights, but at Mr. Adler's words, they turned those off too.

The room was plunged into darkness. The streetlight outside was still glowing, a little beacon in the dark, but a mist was creeping in from the creek.

"Look," Mr. Adler said, low-voiced. "The Brewsters' lights are on."

"Can't be the power lines, then, can it, Roger?" Brian's dad whispered back. "That would get the whole neighborhood."

Mr. Adler nodded. "If it's just this house—then someone threw the breaker in the basement."

All their heads swiveled to the basement door, which stood in the corner of the living room. The door was shut, of course, like it always was. Ollie had shown Brian and Coco around down there once. The floor was rock. The walls stony. It was damp and dim. *Dug in the seventeen hundreds,* Ollie had said proudly. *When the house was first built.*

"You think someone threw the breaker?" Ms. Zintner

said. "No. Surely not." But she was staring at the basement door. They all were.

"I don't hear anything," Mr. Adler said, after a pause. It was pretty easy, in the Egg, to hear things in the basement. Ollie had shown them the old floor grate between it and the ground floor. A relic, Ollie had explained, from the days when a giant woodstove in the basement had heated the house.

Then Brian heard a *thump*. The adults looked at each other.

Clomp.

It sounded like feet on the stairs.

Thud.

Mr. Adler said, "Kids, go upstairs, right now. Amelia, Anne"—he meant Brian's mom and Phil's mom—"Zelda, will you go up with the kids? Keep trying the police. Go into my bedroom. It has a lock on the door."

Brian's mom nodded once. "Come on. Up the stairs," she said briskly. "Anne, can you carry Mikey? Phil, you first, get your crutches."

"I—" Brian tried.

Crack went a foot on the basement stairs.

"Now, baby," his mom said. Mrs. Greenblatt was already heading for the stairs with Mikey in her arms.

Mr. Adler had gone to the rack of cast-iron fire tools sitting next to the empty woodstove. "Here." He handed the heavy iron shovel to Brian's dad, and the poker to Mr. Greenblatt. He took the tongs.

Mrs. Greenblatt and Mikey were at the top of the stairs already. Phil was halfway up, thumping awkwardly on his crutches. Brian and Coco were behind him, hesitating. Brian didn't want to just leave the dads to deal with it. He didn't even know what *it* was. His mom and Ms. Zintner were on the stairs below, urging him up.

"Go!" snapped his mother and Ms. Zintner together, just as the footsteps stopped on the other side of the basement door. Transfixed, Brian watched the knob turn. Watched the door swing slowly open. Saw a dark shape in the doorway. Brian switched on his headlamp.

Everyone froze.

Brian, astonished, saw baggy clothes in a sickly swirl of colors. Huge red shoes. Bony white hands, with long, pointed fingernails, spread in a *ta-da* pose in the doorway. A huge, red-painted mouth smiling. Needle-thin teeth.

Mrs. Greenblatt shrieked. The clown mimed applause. Its eyes were yellow and unblinking.

A dainty tap came on the French doors. Another clown stood outside. It gave Brian a coy little wave. Its nails were two inches long. Brian's mom shook off her shock. "Get up the stairs!" she snapped, backing up. Ms. Zintner was right next to her.

Below them, the clown from the basement had begun

crossing the living room with an exaggerated, cartoon-character tiptoe, fingers crooked like claws. Heading straight toward their dads, guarding the stairwell with the fire tools.

Mr. Adler bellowed, "Stop!" but the clown didn't. Mr. Adler stepped forward and swung the tongs, just as Brian's dad swung the shovel. Mr. Greenblatt hadn't moved. He looked paralyzed with fear.

Both fire tools connected with a *clang*, vibrating. The clown reeled in a circle, a hand to its forehead. Brian thought for sure it was going down.

But as it turned, its eyes fell on Brian, and it *winked*. Like it was doing a circus pratfall.

"Dad, get out of there!" Brian screamed. "Mr. Adler! You can't hurt it, you need to run, come on!"

The clown gave a little bow. Then it reached out and tapped the frozen Mr. Greenblatt on the cheek. The fire poker fell from Mr. Greenblatt's hands. "Dad!" cried Phil from the top of the stairs.

Brian didn't know what had happened. His brain didn't process it. His brain wasn't *made* to process it, maybe. Just, where Mr. Greenblatt had been was—something small, huddled on the floor.

The clown picked it up tenderly while they all stood frozen in horror. Tucked a Mr. Greenblatt–shaped doll into its pocket. Smiled at them all.

There was a crash of glass. Their stunned eyes all went to the French doors. The clown there had broken one of the panes. It put a hand to its mouth with a wide-eyed expression of *oops*. Then it reached in, turned the door handle, and strolled into the living room. It waved at the first clown, who waved back.

Mrs. Greenblatt was screaming continuously. All the rest of the grown-ups were backing up. "Up the stairs!" Mr. Adler yelled, and then Phil was stumping up the rest of the way, as fast as his crutches could take him. Brian and Coco were right behind him, and his mom and Coco's were below that. His dad and Mr. Adler hoisted their fire tools again, right at the foot of the staircase.

"Don't let them touch you!" Coco screamed. "Whatever you do—"

"Dad!" Brian cried. Coco's mom, he saw, was trying her phone, uselessly, one more time.

Now the two clowns stood in front of the two dads guarding the stairs. One of them started waving its fists and hopping back and forth, like a parody of boxing.

Brian and Coco were at the top of the stairwell by then, with Phil behind them. Brian could hear Mikey crying. "Dad, come on!" Brian cried. "Please!"

His dad swung the shovel at the hopping clown. Mr. Adler whacked the other with the tongs. The heavy fire tools bounced off. But this time, one of the clowns gave them an exaggerated frown. It wagged a long-nailed finger. *Ah-ah-ah.* Then it reached out, grabbed both of the fire tools, and dragged both dads forward.

It happened so fast. The second clown reached out and tapped them on the head. And they were falling. Brian swallowed back vomit. "Dad?" he whispered, just as his mom screamed, "Win!" Without looking back, she snapped at Brian, "Baby, get in that room *right now*. Come on, up the stairs."

Ms. Zintner was backing up too. Brian could see her shake. "Roger," she said. "Roger."

The clowns had collected the two new dolls. Tucked them in their pockets. Then they looked up the stairs. They looked at each other. One made an elaborate gesture at the other. *After you.* The other waved its hands. *No, after you.*

Then they faced the stairwell and started to tiptoe up together. Their pockets bulged. Their shoes thumped on the stairs. Their teeth were as yellow as their eyes. Brian was in the doorway of Mr. Adler's room, with Coco beside him. The clowns were climbing faster and faster.

"Mom!" he and Coco shouted together. He saw his mom and Ms. Zintner exchange a look of understanding. Brian didn't get it.

"Shut the door, baby," said his mom.

Then his mom and Ms. Zintner each took a running

step forward and tackled the two clowns back down the stairs. He heard the thumping as they fell. Coco screamed.

"Get in here!" Phil bellowed from behind.

Brian was sobbing as he slammed the bedroom door. Coco was too. They all were. Phil tried to turn on the light, but it was dead. Brian locked the door and began shoving a bureau in front of it. Coco helped him, straining. They got the bureau in place just as the door rattled from the outside. The bureau lurched, but it was heavy. It held. They heard the thumping steps as the clown went farther down the hallway. Maybe looking for another way in. There wasn't one, though. Just the window.

Mrs. Greenblatt had sunk down on the bed with Mikey in her arms.

"Oh God," she whispered. "Oh God, oh God."

"What was it, Phil?" Mikey whimpered. "What is it?"

"It's—" Phil obviously didn't know what to say. "It's gonna be okay, Mikey."

Brian leaned on the bureau for a second. He didn't know what to do. Coco stood beside him, shaking, her face tear-streaked. She obviously didn't know either.

"Mom?" Mikey said. "Mom, are you okay? Mommy?"

His voice quivered. Phil spun around, staggering on his crutches. He shined his headlamp at the bed. Brian turned too. Coco gasped.

Mrs. Greenblatt was sitting bolt upright and perfectly

rigid on the bed. Her eyes were open, unblinking. And wrapped around her ankle, right above her bare foot, right below the hem of her blue summer skirt, was a long-nailed white hand, reaching out from under the bed.

Phil lunged for his mom and little brother, but the white hand was faster. It went up, groping like some kind of white spider, and grabbed Mikey by the foot. Mikey turned huge eyes up to Phil's face. "Phil?" he said. "I'm so *stiff*, Phil."

And just like that, both of them—Mikey and Mrs. Greenblatt—were crumpling, then *gone*, and there were two perfect dolls lying there on the bed.

Phil was yelling incoherently, dropping his crutches. But Coco leaped forward and dragged him back, just as a grinning clown face peered triumphantly out from under the bed. Its smile was bleached to bone and black blood in the swinging white light of their headlamps. Coco and Phil lurched back against the wall as a leg and an arm appeared, and the clown began to wriggle out.

"Help me!" Brian snapped. He was trying as hard as he could to shove the bureau away from the door, his shoulders straining. Phil helped him, grunting, gasping at the pain in his ankle.

"There's two outside!" Coco panted.

The clown from under the bed rolled to its feet, dusting itself off.

With a yell of pure rage, Brian whipped around and threw the only thing at hand—the glass of water on Mr. Adler's nightstand—right at it.

He hit it full in the face with a gout of water.

And—the clown stopped. Its grinning face started to smear as the water ran down it. Just like makeup that had gotten wet. Scarlet drips from the mouth, black lines from its eyes. But—there wasn't anything under the makeup. Like the clown was a kid's chalk painting, dissolving in the rain. Its eyes dripped down its face in a black-and-yellow smear. Its mouth ran down its chin.

The clown spun in a circle, hissing. Brian thought, *It's blind, it's blind now.*

"Wow," said Coco.

But they weren't out of danger. The clown started groping around the room for them. Brian grabbed the blanket at the foot of the bed and threw it over the thing, trapping its arms, and then he kicked it down onto the bed. Then he grabbed the cup, dashed into Mr. Adler's bathroom. Filled the cup. The clown on the bed was already getting up.

Coco had opened the door a crack. "I don't see the other two clowns," she whispered. "Brian, what do you think? How do we get out of here?"

Behind them, there was a thud as the blind clown staggered to its feet and started clawing at the blanket over its head. They couldn't stay where they were.

"We can't stay in this room. Guest room across the hall," whispered Brian. "I'll go first." He hoisted the glass of water.

Coco nodded. Brian went out. His heartbeat seemed to rattle his whole body. A glass of water didn't feel like much of a weapon. He looked up and down the dark hall. Where were the clowns? His headlamp created a tunnel effect where anything in the beam was brightly lit and the shadows on either side seemed darker. Behind him, he heard Phil thumping across the hall. Heard Coco's footsteps beside him. He looked down the stairs. Saw a white face at the foot of the stairs, just turning around.

Coco screamed, "Brian!"

He didn't think. He just whirled and flung the water full on the other clown, which had almost sneaked up on him from the far end of the hall. Then Brian dove into the guest room. Coco slammed the door a second before one of the clowns hit it, rattling the knob. It took them all to shut it. This door didn't lock. And there wasn't a heavy bureau to push in front of it.

Brian still had his water glass. But it was empty. And the guest room didn't have an attached bathroom. The clown outside slammed into the door again. Brian and Phil held it shut while Coco hastily looked around the room, shining her headlamp in corners, under the bed. No sign of more clowns.

But they were trapped.

Now Coco ran to the window. Looked down. Bit her lip. "There's the big trellis," she said. "We could maybe climb down." She twisted her hands together.

"No way," Brian said. "Phil can't do it. We're sticking together."

Phil's face was so white, every freckle stood out like a spot of ink. He said, "Someone has to stay behind anyway. To hold the door shut. And you guys have to get out. How are you supposed to beat the smiling man and fix this if you're trapped in the house?"

Brian and Coco were silent. Phil was shaking like a leaf. He had been turned into a scarecrow back in October. Brian knew that he still woke up with nightmares of it. "What are you waiting for?" Phil added. "You'll be on bikes for an hour to get to the carnival, *and* you need to stop at my house in town. Are you hearing me? You need to grab the water guns. They're in the garage. Some serious Wicked Witch of the West vibes, huh?"

A massive shove pushed them back from the door, and a white hand came groping into the room, a slice of yellow eye and the gleam of teeth just beyond. Phil shoved back, pushing as hard as he could. "Go!" he cried. "And when you see Ollie, tell her that I just beat her in the big hero department."

"Phil," Brian said helplessly. "Phil, come on."

"He's right, Brian," Coco whispered. "We have to get out of here, we have to, we have to win, we have to fix this." She sounded like she was crying. She crossed the room, shoved the window up, unlatched the screen, let it fall. "Brian, come on."

The doorknob to the guest bedroom was rattling. Coco hoisted herself out the window, started to climb down. Brian, swallowing, followed her. "Phil—" he said. He had his feet on the trellis, his hands on the sill.

"Go!" snarled Phil.

Brian heard the guest room door fly open. Heard the sound of a *thunk*—maybe crutches hitting a clown face. Then Phil screamed. Heavy steps ran toward the window. Brian started climbing down as fast as he could.

Coco dropped to the ground, staggered, kept her feet. "Brian—*jump!*" she cried, and he did, falling into Mr. Adler's neglected flower beds and rolling. A clown face thrust out of the window. It wasn't smiling now.

"Bikes in the garage," Brian said. He was already sprinting around the house. Coco was on his tail. They wrenched open the garage side door, and Coco pushed the button to open the big doors. Ollie's purple Schwinn showed clear in their headlamps, right next to Mr. Adler's bigger bike. Brian hoped that Mr. Adler had oiled the chain and kept air in the tires on the Schwinn. Brian bent, fingers scrabbling, and pressed the rubber. Seemed okay. "Coco, take Ollie's," he said. She grabbed it just as he turned and seized Mr. Adler's. The two of them wrenched the bikes around and ran out of the garage just as the first clown burst out of the house, not bothering to sneak, just running.

But Brian and Coco were already pedaling, hardly noticing their bare feet. No time to grab shoes. They shot down the driveway, turned left, tires squealing, and picked up speed. The clown was left behind in the summer dust, and they pedaled on into a tunnel of darkness, with only the light of their headlamps to show the way.

14

DURING THE DAY, the funhouse resembled any other carnival funhouse, except it was cooler. You walked through its winding halls and galleries. A bright green exit sign glowed just ahead. The giggles of families echoed off the mirrors. There were mirrors on all sides. Walls. Ceiling. Floor. The mirrors distorted your reflection. Sometimes they made you taller. Sometimes shorter. Sometimes basketball-shaped, sometimes skinny, with an S curve to your middle. Sometimes you'd be pinheaded or bug-eyed.

When Ollie went into the funhouse this time, it seemed just the same. The sounds of people laughing still echoed off the walls. The sound of carnival music slid brightly through the corridors. The mirrors still turned her into a thousand strangers.

Ollie wondered why the smiling man wouldn't go into the funhouse. If she didn't know better, she'd have thought that he was afraid. But what did he, of all people, have to be afraid of? She hoped she'd never know what he was afraid of.

She started walking. Came to some mirrored steps, just like she would have in the daytime. She recognized a smudge on one mirror. A thin crack in another.

Down more steps. Through a narrow passage. She could still hear the carnival music. Wherever you went in the carnival, the music followed.

Then the path widened into a round room, where the mirrors almost seemed to—smear her reflection somehow. Then the way angled sharply left and started to climb up in a spiral. Around and around.

Now Ollie realized that she could no longer hear the sounds of other people. Just the squeak of her sneakers on the mirrored floor, the huff of her breath, and the constant music.

She didn't recognize this part of the funhouse. Maybe she was getting somewhere . . .

Thunk. An odd noise came from up ahead.

Ollie's steps faltered.

Thunk.

Ollie imagined monsters. Something horrible enough to frighten the smiling man. She swerved, tried a new direction, walking faster. *Thunk*, closer now, still ahead of her. Like she'd never changed direction. She spun again, diving right down a T-junction. *Thunk.* Closer than ever. Before she could decide what to do, a person came into view. A grown-up. He was making the noise, Ollie realized. He was thumping his head against the mirror in front of him.

Thunk. Thump.

Ollie ran forward. "Hey," she said. "Hey, what are you doing? You'll hurt yourself!"

He ignored her.

"Hey, mister, *stop!*" Ollie put a hand on his shoulder.

The man looked up. He wasn't bleeding or cut or even bruised from thumping his head against the mirror. His face was gray. The skin drooped around his eyes and mouth, and his eyes were sunk and shrunken like raisins.

Ollie recoiled. She'd met ghosts before.

"Can't," the man whispered, and let his head fall forward again. *Thunk.* "Can't stop." *Thunk.* "I'll hear them if I stop. I'll see them." *Thunk.* "Don't want to. Can't stand it." *Thunk.*

"Who will you hear? Who will you see?"

But either he wouldn't say or he couldn't. He didn't say anything else. Finally Ollie turned away and fled up the passageway.

The music played on. Ollie trembled. *How many ghosts are in here? Did he just—could he not find the way out? What can't he stand?*

She bit her lips and kept on. Was it her imagination, or was the light getting dimmer?

Something moved in the mirror on her left. Ollie spun to face it, saw nothing but her own pale face. She ran on. Tried to keep her head. Tried to think where the second key might be, tried to look for keyholes where she could try the first key. She saw a black streak on a mirror about twenty feet ahead. Hurried toward it.

But it wasn't a keyhole. Or a secret door. Someone had written *LET ME OUT* on the mirror in sprawling grease-pencil letters.

Ollie put a hand on her mouth, turned away from the writing, chose another passage. Her heartbeat seemed to shake her whole body. *Keep going, Ollie.*

Now Ollie saw a billow of flame in the mirror. She turned around with a gasp, expecting to see fire in the corridor behind her. Nothing. Then she heard a scream. She turned back to the mirror.

Saw fire reflected in its depths. But not fire in the funhouse. It was a fire from Ollie's head. From her dreams. Ollie saw a whole scene, dim in the glass. A small plane burning in an empty field. Black trees framing the horizon.

It hadn't happened that way, of course. They told Ollie her mom had died right away. That it hadn't hurt. But of course, that had never been what Ollie imagined.

"Mom?" she whispered to the mirror. *"Mom?"*

No answer. Just the fire straight out of her nightmares. Ollie turned away, a fist in her mouth, trying to think. *Look for keyholes, Ollie. Come on.*

But after only a few steps, she heard a loud rustling. She looked up again. Now she saw corn reflected in the mirrors. Corn dead with autumn, gray and rustling, taller than her head, silhouetted against a gray autumn sky.

And above that, two scarecrows propped over the corn. Their faces were burlap and straw. Their mouths had been sewn on. But Ollie recognized them anyway. Coco and Brian. You couldn't mistake Coco's pinkish-blond hair, even if it was done in yarn. Or Brian's beautiful smile, even if it was done with thread. She'd failed them. The smiling man had turned them into scarecrows, and they'd sit there, guarding a dead cornfield, forever . . .

As Ollie watched, the two scarecrows in the mirror looked at her and gave sad little waves.

Ollie sprinted away. She couldn't stand it anymore. *That's what this place is. It shows you your worst fears. Is that why the smiling man won't come in?*

How do I get out? She didn't know. She was trapped. As she ran, she imagined she could hear the smiling man's voice in her ears.

Didn't I warn you, Olivia?

15

THEY HAD TO go down Farm Hill Road to get back into the main part of Evansburg. Farm Hill Road was really steep, but Brian didn't dare slow down. He didn't know if the clowns marched like zombies, or had a clown car, or honestly flew like bats. They had to get to the carnival.

He shot down Farm Hill Road at a hideously unsafe speed, and Coco was right on his tail. Ordinarily Coco didn't love going fast and would have screamed her head off. But she just clenched her hands on the handlebars, hunched her shoulders against the hot wind of their speed, and didn't say anything.

They got to the bottom with no sign of clowns, and Brian made the left onto Bank Street that would take them to Phil's. He tried not to think of his last sight of Phil. Being sad or scared wouldn't help right now. They had to *win*.

"I'm sorry, Brian," Coco said suddenly.

Brian had been calculating in his head. *An hour out to the carnival, water guns in the garage, we need shoes . . .* Coco interrupted his planning. "What?"

"The smiling man told me that, if I decided to play, then this was what would happen. That he'd get everyone. And he did." Coco's voice shook.

"Don't you dare say it's your fault," Brian said. His last memory of his parents, of Phil, of Mikey's terrified face, kept playing on a loop in his head, even though he was trying to be brave. "We're just kids. This was always too big and too strange for us. We're just doing our best. You want Ollie back. I do too. We're going to get her back. We're going to get *everyone* back. And we're going to do it together."

Coco was quiet for a second. Then she huffed out a laugh. "Thanks," she said. "I really needed to hear that."

"It's all true," Brian said, and they braked their bikes in front of Philip Greenblatt's empty house.

———

Phil's water pistols weren't huge, but they were better than nothing. Brian filled them at the hose outside, while Coco kept an eye on the road. But nothing stirred. Brian could hear a TV going in the house next door. Once he heard an owl call. Another time they heard a wild, inhuman chuckle. Coco looked terrified, but Brian said, "Fox," and went on filling water pistols. They saw no evidence of clowns at all.

Finally, with the water pistols tucked securely in the basket on Ollie's bike, they stole some sneakers and set off again.

Coco obviously felt bad stealing Mikey's beloved T. rex Keds—the only ones that would fit her. Brian, tying Phil's favorite Nikes, said only, "He wouldn't mind."

Coco's eyes were wet again. But all she said was "I guess he wouldn't." She was staring down the road to where her own house—and shoes that fit better—waited, but Brian said, "We should go. It's another hour bike ride out to the fairgrounds."

And Coco's house would be as dark and empty as Phil's, he thought but didn't say. Coco got on Ollie's bike without a word, and they pedaled out of town.

The wind was hot and swampy in Brian's face. It dried his tears. Main Street was ghostly in the moonlight. They pedaled cautiously. Neither of them was crying anymore. Urgency and adrenaline had shut all that out. There was only what was in front of them. Their tires hissed: a sound like rain on the asphalt. There was no other sound. No crickets, no peepers.

But—

"Do you hear that?" Coco said.

Brian strained his ears, and after a second or two, he did. Music. It drifted on the wind: thin and tinny, but unmistakable. Carnival music.

"Yeah. Do you smell it?" Brian whispered back. His throat felt parched. His voice was a breathless thread.

He saw her breathe in. "Yeah," she said, and made a face.

It smelled like cotton candy and fried dough and soda. But there was something off about it, as though all the carnival food had sat out for three days in the rain and started to spoil.

They pedaled over the Main Street Bridge that spanned the creek, past the green on the edge of the Evansburg waterfall, and soon afterward the asphalt became dirt, hard-packed and bone-dry in the rainless, breathless heat. The dust rose up from their tires. It was awfully dark. They both had their headlamps on, sweeping the ground in front of them.

Brian wasn't sure what time it was. They were out of Evansburg by then, surrounded by fields thick with green corn that stood massed and still in the humid night. The music had gotten louder, shrill and discordant. Cars occasionally passed them on the road. Brian wondered if someone would stop and ask them what they were doing, but no one did.

"There's the carnival," Coco whispered, and they braked their bikes to look. The ripe corn sliced up their view of it so that Brian, straining his eyes, saw the thing only in pieces.

But even the pieces were impressive. Lights traced the arc of the Ferris wheel, swirled like a maelstrom around the Tilt-A-Whirl. Above all those things stood a giant statue of a clown, smiling broadly, with teeth square as tombstones.

He took a deep breath. "Let's do this," he said.

Then Brian heard a car. The back of his neck prickled. Instinct, but he trusted it. "Get off the road!" he cried.

Coco trusted him too. She swerved her bike into the corn. They turned off their headlamps and lay flat against the ground with the corn rustling overhead. A tiny clown car zoomed by.

It passed them and kept going. Brian let out a breath.

Then the car stopped. Brian froze. The car reversed. Slowly, slowly, the car drove backward. A tiny door opened in the tiny car, and a clown got out. Brian didn't think it could see them. They were deep in the shadows. Could it—smell them? Brian had a water pistol in his hand, but he was reluctant to use it. He didn't want to waste the water. Maybe there wouldn't be anywhere to refill it.

The clown sniffed. Sniffed again. Turned its head. Its

mouth twitched. Then it started tiptoeing along the road, sniffing the whole time.

"Let's leave the bikes," breathed Brian. "Back into the corn, and we can lose them and run the rest of the way."

Coco nodded. They slid, rustling, back into the corn.

It was dark, and stifling, inside the cornfield. They didn't dare turn their headlamps back on. The corn hadn't been plowed down to make a maze or anything. There was no obvious way through the stalks. Just a constant ducking and shoving, the leaves and stems whipping their faces and arms. Brian had a death grip on Coco's hand, and she was holding tightly on to him too. It would have been so easy to lose each other in the dark.

It was hard to know which sounds were pursuing footsteps and what was just the rustle of corn. Their breathing seemed *ungodly* loud. Had they been spotted?

Then Brian saw the gleam of a smile amid the stalks. Right in front of them, striped black with the shadows of cornstalks. It opened its mouth and lunged. Coco yelped and Brian barely got it with his squirt gun in time. Its face started to smear, eyes blurring into horrible drooping streaks, mouth running red off its chin. But it kept coming, mouth wide, hands groping.

"Come on!" Brian cried to Coco, yanking her to the side. The clown's fingernails almost snagged on his T-shirt.

He swung his headlamp back and forth, saw other white faces closing in.

A stitch was forming between his ribs. They kept running, gasping for air. Ahead of them, the carnival was getting bigger and brighter. The corn was thinning now. The lights of the carnival showed clearly through the stalks. Then they burst out of the corn, gasping, sprinting, and ran into the crowded parking lot.

It looked just like the carnival from any other year, except bigger. More beautiful. And the carnival gate was shaped like a giant red smile. People were flowing in and out. Of course, Brian thought. This was why Evansburg had been so quiet. It was county fair night. Brian wished passionately that everything was normal, that he was just showing up at the annual carnival with his friend Coco. Ollie and Phil would be waiting somewhere on the midway. They'd eat too much junk food and the biggest danger would be that someone would barf in his lap on the Tilt-A-Whirl.

Ha. If only.

A single figure stood still just inside the gate. The lights of the carnival sparkled on his fair hair, but you couldn't see his face at all, with so much brightness behind him.

Coco was still holding Brian's hand. Her grip tightened.

"It's him, isn't it?" Brian said.

"Yeah," Coco said.

"Good evening," said the smiling man. He was wearing jeans and a T-shirt with a wide-winged angel on it that read LED ZEPPELIN. He had his hands stuck in his pockets.

"We're here for Ollie," Brian said.

"And our families," Coco added.

"Not here to see my carnival?" said the smiling man. "How sad. When I sent an escort for you and everything."

"An escort?" demanded Brian. "Do you mean the clowns that . . ." Words failed him.

"Yes, of course," said the smiling man briskly. "Did they get carried away? Unfortunate. They're a bit like hunting dogs with a sense of humor. I put them onto you at the parade. Clever of me, wasn't it?"

His eyes were bright. Neither Coco nor Brian said anything. Brian heard a horn honking behind him and turned. The little clown car had pulled up. Three clowns got out, mouths turned down. One of them had a smeared face. Brian gripped his water pistol tightly.

The smiling man gave the clowns a cold look. Each clown tried to hide behind the other. "I'll deal with you later," the smiling man said to the clowns, and then turned back to Brian and Coco. "Well, even if the escort missed the mark, I'm sure you'll enjoy my carnival regardless."

"I doubt it," Brian said.

"Manners, Brian," said the smiling man.

Coco said, "How do we get Ollie back? And our families?"

"Oh, that," the smiling man said, like it had slipped his mind. "Open the gates by sunrise, and everything will be right as rain. Fail—and the gates never open again. Not for you, not for anyone you love."

Brian and Coco exchanged glances. The summer nights were short. Brian wasn't even sure what time it was.

"When you say right as rain," Coco said, "that means that we and everyone else who is here against their will— everyone—walks free. Is that right?"

"I suppose." It was hard to see the smiling man's expression with the lights so bright at his back.

Coco was standing still, her eyes intent on the smiling man's face. It was the same expression she'd worn when she won the middle school chess championship, Brian thought. Concentrating. Balancing out probabilities. He waited.

Finally, Coco turned to Brian. Low-voiced, she said, "A chance to save everyone, against a chance of being kidnapped ourselves. What do you think?"

"We go for it," Brian said, without hesitation.

Coco still looked like she was thinking hard.

"I have one condition," she said, turning back to the smiling man.

Both brows lifted. "Haggling is unbecoming," he told her. "What makes you think I even want to bargain?"

"Because this is fun for you," Coco said. "You want to see what we'll do. Besides, you can't even talk about *unbecoming*. You're pretending to be a carnival barker while playing games with people's lives. That's unbecoming."

"You'll make the loveliest doll," he informed her, with a touch of malice. "Pretty. *Quiet.*"

Coco glared and said, "This is my condition: You answer any three questions truthfully before we come in."

His eyes narrowed. "One question."

"Two."

"One," he said. "Or don't play at all."

She chewed her lip. Looked at Brian. And then nodded. "Where are the three keys?" she asked the smiling man.

He raised an eyebrow. "Of all the useless questions."

"Fine," Coco said. "If it's so useless, then answer it." Brian really hoped that Coco knew what she was doing.

"One is in a pocket," said the smiling man at last. "One is in a music box. And one does not exist, except in the presence of the other two. Is that sufficient?"

Brian and Coco looked at each other. "Yes," Coco said. "I guess so."

"Then come in," said the smiling man.

16

COCO WAS STILL sweaty from the bike ride. Her legs burned from pedaling. Her head felt stuffed and snotty from crying. Together she and Brian stepped through the gate. The music seemed to reach out and gather them in. The lights flashed red and green. There were people everywhere. It was hard to see over all the heads, hard to hear over the noise of the crowd. Most of Evansburg was there. Coco saw Mr. Easton holding a giant tub of popcorn, saw Jenna Gehrmann in line for the Ferris wheel. The noise seemed to beat on her brain. For a split second she felt foolish, standing there dusty and sweaty and scared next to Brian, holding a sloshing water pistol in one hand, while hundreds of people milled around without a care in the world. No one even glanced at them.

A creak behind them made both Brian and Coco spin

back. The mouth-shaped gate was closing, its two halves coming shut like someone taking a giant bite. The smiling man had disappeared.

"What were the words again?" Coco asked, scanning the midway. The crowd made it hard to see much. "Three words, three keys? Ghost. Mirror. Gate? And he said there was one in a pocket, one in a music box, and—"

"And one doesn't exist except in the presence of the other two," Brian said. "But where do we start looking?"

They had moved away from the gate, their backs to the carnival fence, trying to take everything in. Still, no one in the crowd took any notice of them, even though Coco recognized a bunch of people. Mike Campbell, one of Brian's teammates from hockey, walked within five feet of them both. He didn't turn his head. "Can they even see us?" Coco said in puzzlement.

Brian bit his lip, and then he yelled, "Hey, Mike! Mike!"

Mike kept on walking. Didn't even twitch. "Guess they can't," Brian said. He shivered. Coco didn't blame him. It was eerie, your friends staring straight through you.

Coco tapped a girl on the shoulder. The girl didn't react. "Okay," Coco said. "So there are a lot of people here, but basically we're on our own. Where should we—?"

Brian grabbed her arm. "Look."

Coco saw a long-chinned white face, a red smile, there and gone in the crowd. Turned her head. Another. Closer.

"What do you want to bet *they* can't see us?" Brian whispered.

"Wouldn't take that bet." Coco gripped her water pistol tighter. It seemed like such a shoddy weapon against those huge grins. Then the guy nearest them in the crowd turned around, and it was another clown, *right there*. Coco yelped. Brian reflexively squirted it in the face. It recoiled, hissing, eyes already beginning to drip. Then Brian and Coco ran, ducking and twisting, hampered by the people who couldn't see them, scanning for monsters in the crowd.

"We need to make a plan!" Coco said. It was hard to plan when the world was reduced to a packed crowd, and blaring music, and sharp smiles turned to snarls, creeping closer. She was terrified one of the clowns would get close enough to touch, sneaking through the crowd. She looked around wildly. "The Ferris wheel! We can get high enough to see everything. And the clowns can't get up there unless they can fly."

Midnight, roared a voice from the midway. *HA HA HA.* A giant clown statue, holding a clock, had roared out the hour. How had it gotten so late so fast? Clowns seemed to be everywhere all of a sudden. There was the Ferris wheel platform. Two seats on each car.

"There's a clown on the platform," Coco said.

"No big," Brian said, with bravado. He hefted his water pistol. They sprinted up the steps. The clowns were converging. The crowd was oblivious. The clown on the platform leered at them, reaching out, but Brian's water pistol got it right in the face. Coco cheered, ducked around the people at the front of the line, and got on the next car herself. "Brian!" she called, just as the car began to move. He swerved, sprinting, and jumped on with her just as the car left the platform. They pulled down the safety bar, leaving a bunch of people blinking in confusion and one clown staring up at them, unnoticed by the crowd, its face half melted.

"Okay," Brian said after a moment, when he'd gotten his breath back. "That's better. Now what?"

Coco was already craning around to look at the fair. She saw a Tilt-A-Whirl, a mirrored funhouse. The giant clown in the midway. Booths for games. All of it was growing smaller as their car rose into the sky. There was a fence around the whole carnival, and outside that, nothingness. Just a sea of roiling mist. Coco said, "Look—over there. The sign on that building. It says haunted house."

Brian was scanning the midway far below. Counting the heads of clowns, Coco assumed. "You think we should start there?" he said. "Because the first word is *ghost*?"

"Got a better idea?"

"No." Brian's knuckles were white on his water pistol. "We'll sprint for it the second we're on the ground, okay?" He peered down again. "The clowns are gone. I can't see them."

"What?" Coco looked down herself. It was true. The frizzy red hair and the bright clothes were distinctive, and she couldn't see any of them either. "Do you think they—?"

THUD. The Ferris wheel shuddered. The ground seemed to shake. The whole *carnival* seemed to shake. "Brian, what was that?"

"I don't—"

THUD came the sound again. Coco felt the vibrations in the Ferris wheel. She looked down again. Looking for fireworks or collapsed booths or . . .

"Coco," Brian whispered.

"I don't—"

"*Coco,*" Brian said more forcefully. He jabbed her in the ribs with an elbow. He was twisted around in their seat, looking at something behind them. Coco started to turn just as the huge clown from the midway let out a booming laugh: *HA HA HA.*

Except the laugh wasn't coming from the midway. It was coming from behind them.

Slowly, Coco turned. Saw teeth like tombstones. Red

hair taller than the Ferris wheel. And a giant hand coming up, making a circle with a white thumb and forefinger. Like a kid about to flick a bug.

The hand descended. Coco had a brief, horrifying vision of them being flung backward into space, crashing to the hard, dusty ground like broken dolls—and then *becoming* broken dolls, for the smiling man to laugh at.

"Brian—" Coco breathed, but there was nowhere to go. They were fifty feet up, at the apex of the Ferris wheel. The wheel had stopped moving. A glance down showed a clown at the controls. Grinning. They were trapped. The hand was still descending.

Coco thought fast. "Brian, how good were you at the fireman's pole on the playground?"

"What?"

"I think we can slide down the spoke." Coco pointed at their feet, hoping against hope that it was true. "All the way to the hub in the middle. Better than staying here." The giant fingernail was almost on them. It seemed to fill up the whole world. "We have to try it!" cried Coco.

"Go! Go!" Brian shouted. The lights of the carnival twinkled at their feet. Music and laughter seemed to drown the thunder of Coco's breathing, the working of her heart.

Coco reached for the spoke of the Ferris wheel, wrapped hands and feet around it, and slid down as fast as she dared.

It hurt. It hurt a *lot*. Friction from the metal pole burned her hands and the insides of her knees. But she kept on sliding, tears in her eyes, until she landed with a thump on the hub of the wheel and scrambled sideways, trying to clear a space for Brian, who landed, gasping, a few seconds later. They both looked up. The huge clown looked bewildered. In other circumstances it would have been almost funny.

"We can't stay here," Coco said. "Down the rest of the way? And then run for the haunted house?" She'd shoved her squirt gun into her back jeans pocket before she started sliding. She felt for it. Thankfully, it was still there. Her hands throbbed.

"Yeah," Brian said. "Go!" The clown had aimed a kick at the Ferris wheel. Coco could see the giant red shoe . . .

She grabbed the spoke below the hub, gritted her teeth, and slid the rest of the way to the ground. Brian was right behind her. The both screamed all the way. The Ferris wheel spokes were a *lot* longer than the fireman's pole in the playground. She felt the skin blistering on her palms. They hit the lowermost car, and then jumped back onto the platform, just as a kick struck the hub where they'd been.

But they were already jumping off the platform, holding their water guns, trying to see white clown faces in the masses of people. "Do you think," Brian panted as they ran, "that Mr. Easton and Mike and those guys just don't *notice* that a giant clown is stamping around the carnival, kicking stuff?"

WHAM. A giant foot in a giant red shoe dropped ten feet from Coco's elbow, and she yelped and veered away. It was trying to *step* on them. Like they were bugs.

We're behind the mist, Coco thought, dragging in air. *We're outside the rest of the world, somehow, that's why they can't see us . . .*

That's what she thought. But all she said was "Talk less, run more!"

And then they were running, scrabbling, trying not to get crushed under that impossible shoe.

"Which way?" Coco said. Brian had a better sense of direction than she did.

"Left of the ring toss," Brian gasped. "Right at the archery, behind concessions, and then turn left again."

"Okay," Coco wheezed.

"Coco!" Brian cried, and pulled her sideways. The foot came down again. She was dripping sweat, scrabbling for purchase in the dry dirt with Mikey Greenblatt's slightly too small sneakers. They ducked behind the concession stand right as the giant scarlet shoe dropped again, this time squarely in front of them. Barring the way to the haunted house.

"Climb over it!" shouted Brian. They hurled themselves up, scrabbling at shoelaces that felt uncanny, somewhere between plastic and rubber and *flesh*. The clown started to pick up its foot just as they got to the top, but they were already sliding down the other side of the shoe. They dodged another kick. The haunted house was coming up on their right.

"Sure about this?" panted Brian.

Everything about the building looked sinister. The peeling façade, the darkness within. Even the way the haunted house sign flickered so that all you could see was HAUNTED. HAUNTED. HUNTED.

"I'm sure," Coco said, and then they darted through the door, slammed it shut on one last wild swing from the giant clown, bumbled through a doorway, and found themselves in darkness.

17

THEY DARTED THROUGH the front door, turning on their headlamps as they did. There were two options. A staircase. And an open door to their left. They couldn't see through the door or up the staircase.

They hesitated.

Then a footstep sounded on the stairs. They looked up. Three clowns on the stairwell, their heads cocked to one side. Delighted red smiles split their faces. Then they raised their crooked fingers and started to run down the stairs.

On instinct, Brian and Coco ducked left, through the open doorway. Coco was a step ahead of Brian. He slammed the door, and then they stood for a second, panting, waiting for the thump on the door as a clown tried to get in.

It didn't come.

Then Coco looked around properly. The lights of their small headlamps swung this way and that. She forgot to breathe.

Faces, everywhere.

Clown faces.

Smiling. Scowling. Drooping. Packed in like firewood. But they weren't moving. Each face—there was something wrong with it. Some were smeared. Some looked like they had been made wrong entirely, with four eyes instead of a nose and mouth, or two mouths where the eyes should be. Or an ear for a nose. Everywhere there was another face, like a slice out of a nightmare. A forest of them. Brian and Coco stood still, their backs to the door.

The clowns didn't move.

"Maybe they're dead?" Coco whispered. "Or—something."

"Look," Brian whispered back. "There at the far end. Look. Another door. We could try getting past those clowns on the stairwell. Or—"

"Cross the room? At least these ones aren't moving."

"Let's go through," Brian said. "Don't let them touch you."

Coco nodded. They started forward. The clowns were packed so closely together that you couldn't just hurry through the room. They had to step gingerly around each sprawling limb, the trembling light of their headlamps showing more and more faces. Needle teeth that came past one clown's chin. An eye that was six inches higher than the other. As they crept by the clowns, Coco could almost *feel* the brush of their clothes. She was trembling harder and harder. But the clowns still didn't move.

Halfway across the room now. Coco paused, shivering, and then realized something. Every clown in the room had turned to face them.

"Brian," Coco whispered.

She didn't see which clown reached out, but suddenly her T-shirt was caught on the sharp prongs of fingernails. She yanked away, gasping.

"Coco!" cried Brian, but he'd been wrapped in long, soft arms. He struggled. Coco's brain writhed in panic for a second, but then she realized that Brian was not turning into a doll. Maybe only the clowns outside could do that.

Brian wrenched himself loose, but then another clown had Coco by the ankle, and slowly, all those drooping, distorted faces were starting to smile . . .

The door they'd come through flew open, and three clowns stood framed in the doorway. They all had the ordinary sorts of eyes and mouths and noses. They mimed polite applause at all the clowns and pieces of clowns around the room.

Then they started to cross the room.

More and more arms were reaching out, grabbing,

trying to hold on to Brian and Coco. Brian was straining to reach his water pistol. Coco wrenched back from the snatching fingers and managed to grab hers. The part clowns fell back from the stream of water. The whole clowns were crossing the room faster, their smiles morphing into frowns. Brian had his arms loose and had snatched his water pistol in turn.

Then they were trying to run, shoving, gasping, with clowns on every side, hitting them with water, hearing a hissing like snakes rise up in their wake. By the thinnest possible margin, they got to the door at the far end, shot through it, and slammed it shut.

"Out of water," Brian said.

"Me too."

They were in a stairwell. The only way was back through the door or up the stairs. At least Coco couldn't see any clowns. They took off running up the stairs. Below, they heard the creak of a door opening, but they didn't turn around. There was a door at the top of the stairs. They clattered through it and stood back to back, expecting more horrors.

What they saw was an old-fashioned living room. They stood still in surprise.

Then Brian said, "Ollie was here, wasn't she?"

Coco nodded. She had the same feeling that Brian did. This room didn't feel like the rest of the carnival. It felt—human, somehow. Even the smell was sort of like Ollie. Coco couldn't have said why.

"Does the door lock?" Brian asked, just as the handle rattled. They both threw themselves at the door with the strength of terror, but they realized quickly that no matter how much the door handle rattled, there was no inward pressure.

They looked at each other, not daring to leave the door, since they were out of water, but wanting to explore the room.

Coco, leaning on the door, was looking around. "What's that?" she said suddenly. Her eye had fallen on a stack of paper on the mantelpiece. They looked like pages torn out of a book.

"Go see?" Brian said. "I'm okay here. It doesn't—doesn't *seem* like they can get in. Which makes sense, doesn't it? That Ollie would have a safe place."

"I hope she would," Coco said with a shudder, and crossed the room to the mantelpiece.

It was a stack of pages torn out of *Alice's Adventures in Wonderland*. Brian frowned at them, letting the door go. It didn't move. "Ollie loves that book," he observed, taking the pages.

"Maybe she didn't tear out the pages, then," Coco said. "No, wait—what are those?"

She and Brian peered closer. Under certain words in the text, someone had made markings with a fingernail.

"Is it a message?" whispered Coco in excitement.

"Dunno," Brian said. He went back to the earliest page and started to read the marked words.

"*Alive. Went fun house*," Brian read. "*They—cannot—get in this room. Love.*" And the last thing marked was an exclamation where Alice said, *Oh!*

Coco realized there were tears in her eyes. She'd tried really hard to be brave and keep faith and stuff. But it had been like chasing a ghost.

"Funhouse," she said, wiping her eyes. "Ollie's in the funhouse."

"And it's safe up here," Brian said. "Thank goodness. Let's see if there's a place to fill the water guns. And I'd really like to pee."

18

OLLIE DIDN'T KNOW how long she'd been in the funhouse. She only knew that she had to keep walking. She wasn't walking out of hope anymore. She wasn't looking for the key. She was out of courage. There was no way out. She'd accepted that. The smiling man hadn't lied. Maybe he really had tried to warn her in his own way. She just walked, because she couldn't stand to stop. She tried not to look into any mirrors.

She couldn't do anything about the voices, though. She tried covering her ears, but she still heard them.

"Psst," whispered Brian from one mirror. He was standing next to Coco, their heads close together. They looked vaguely older. They were talking to each other. "Do you ever think about Ollie anymore?"

Coco said, "Who? Oh, that girl we used to hang out with? Was that her name?"

Ollie hurried past, head down.

"Happy birthday, my beautiful girl," said her dad from another mirror. His voice was just like it always was, full of laughter. "I've got a birthday joke for you: Why do seagulls fly over the ocean?"

Ollie looked up before she could stop herself, and her mirror-dad wasn't talking to Ollie. He was talking to Coco. A Coco who was definitely older. She looked so beautiful. So grown-up. Coco rolled her blue eyes, but she was smiling. "I don't know. Why, Dad?" she said.

"Because if they flew over the bay, we'd call them bagels!" cried her dad, slapping his leg and laughing, and Coco was laughing with him.

Ollie went on. She wasn't crying. At first she'd thought things like, *Okay, that's one of my worst memories*. Like the day her dad came to school to see her and told Ollie her mom was dead. And then she'd think, *Okay, that didn't really happen. That's just one of my greatest fears*. But pretty soon it all started running together in her head—what had happened and what she was scared would happen—until it became one big ball of *everything awful* that her mind contained, imagined or real, thrown up in color and surround sound on those horrible, impervious mirrors. "Ollie," gasped her dad from a new mirror. His face was pale green, his lips black, his whole arm swollen. "I'm sorry, baby, I didn't mean to die. I wanted to be there for you. I did."

Ollie lost it. "That didn't happen!" she screamed at the mirror. "It didn't, it didn't! That's a lie! I saved my dad. I did!"

Ollie ripped off her sneaker and started whaling on the glass for all she was worth, trying to break it. "Stop it!" she screamed at no one. "Stop it! It's not true. It's not real!"

"Ollie," other voices were saying. "Ollie, Ollie."

It was just mirror-Coco and mirror-Brian gossiping about her. "Shut up!" she screamed at the sound of their voices. "Shut up!" No matter how hard she hit it, the glass wouldn't break, the voices wouldn't stop. She'd be walking through the funhouse forever until she was really haunting the carnival, just like her first morning on the midway, when she was scared she was dead.

"*Ollie!*" yelled Brian's and Coco's voices again.

"Go away!" she screamed back at them. "Go away!" She was so lonely.

Footsteps, not hers, pounding. Ollie refused to look. She buried her face in her arms.

Then suddenly there were arms around her, sweaty, dirty arms, and Coco's voice saying, "Ollie, are you okay? Are you okay? Say something."

Brian crushed her in a hug on the other side. "Oh my God," he said, over and over. "Oh my God. We found you. Ollie? Ollie?"

Her friends pulled back and looked at her. And it was

them. It was really them. Ollie stared at them, shocked, almost afraid. It was too close to what she'd imagined. What she'd hoped for and dreamed about. What she'd meant to happen when she left that message in her room. But now she was scared she was just imagining them. That this was a new trick of the funhouse.

"Are you . . ." She licked her lips. "Are you real?"

In answer, they hugged her again, and now all three of them were crying.

"You came," Ollie whispered. "I didn't think you were coming."

"Of course we were," Coco said. "We got your message. Way to go, with the pages. We were always coming. It's just this awful funhouse, making you believe terrible things."

Ollie opened her mouth. Brian and Coco seemed okay. Well, filthy and tense. But okay. "It's—it's not doing it to you? Showing you the worst things? In the mirrors?"

"Oh, it is." Brian pressed his lips together. "But we came through the funhouse together, see? Me and Coco. So whenever the mirror showed one of us something nasty, the other one just said, like, hey, that's imaginary. Or, yeah, maybe that happened, but it's in the past, you're okay now. That's what friends do, after all."

"The smiling man said there was no way out of here," Ollie whispered.

"I bet it's impossible to get through the funhouse *alone*," put in Coco. "But we aren't alone, are we? Not like him."

Ollie burst into tears, and they all hugged again. Brian said, "See? You need us, Ollie. Never leave us behind again, okay?"

Ollie sniffled and rubbed her eyes with the back of her hand. "Okay," she said. "Look." She reached into her pocket. "I have the first key—do you know about the keys?"

Coco's face lit up. "A pocket!" she cried. "That's what he meant. I got the smiling man to answer one question before we agreed to come into the carnival. I asked him where the keys were, and he said the first was in a pocket!"

"Coco, you're brilliant," Ollie said. "Where's the next one?"

"He said in a music box," Brian said. "Is there a music box?"

"Well," said Ollie, thinking. "There's always music. But—wait. Be quiet a second?"

Coco and Brian went quiet. The carnival music, always in the background, played on. Ollie said slowly, "You know, there's always music playing here. But I never knew where it was coming from. You never see speakers or anything."

"Could it be a music box?" Coco said.

"Don't know. But what if we just—follow the sound?" Ollie said.

"Let's do it," Brian said. They all got to their feet.

It still wasn't easy, walking through the funhouse. Images formed in the mirrors, voices shouted at them. They saw awful things. But Brian and Coco were right. It was a lot less scary with your friends. It wouldn't have been possible, Ollie thought, without her friends. They held hands and kept walking.

Until their way dead-ended at a big square mirror, with a keyhole in the middle.

Ollie got out the first key, put it in the lock. Twisted.

The door swung open.

They found themselves in a big octagonal room that none of them had seen before. It was empty except that in the middle was an old-timey music box. It was open. It was playing the exact same tune as the carnival music outside, in a small, sweet chime. They crossed the room together and saw that the music box was empty except for an old-fashioned key. Ollie reached in, carefully, and took it out. Brian, just as carefully, reached over and shut the music box.

And for the first time since Ollie had seen the carnival, the music stopped.

19

THERE WAS ANOTHER keyhole set in the very center of
one of the walls in the octagon room. When Ollie tried the
music box key, it fit. The wall of the octagon swung open,
and none of them was very surprised to see that the way
led straight back out onto the carnival midway.

Ollie wasn't sure how long she'd been in the funhouse,
wasn't sure what time Brian and Coco had found her. But
it *felt* late. Super late. Like the blackest part of the night
after moonset and before dawn.

The carnival was deserted now. Ollie was used to seeing it teem with life. But now there was complete stillness.
Just the movement of an old napkin and an old popcorn
container, blowing in a sudden, sharp breeze.

The smiling man waited next to the front gate. They
walked up to meet him.

Ollie said, "We got out."

"I thought you might," he said. He wasn't smiling. But she'd learned to read his face, all those evenings playing chess. Learned to read when the game was going well or badly, learned to know whether he was going to pin her queen with his lurking knight. This time, she could have sworn he looked pleased. Amused.

"All of you could stay, if you wanted," he said. "I could show you so much."

Ollie shook her head. She pulled out the two keys, the one from the haunted house and the one from the funhouse. Frowning, she brought them near each other. The keys sprang together, quivering, and she was holding one giant key in her hand. *The gate key*, she thought. A murmur ran through the whole carnival. Like the clowns and the dolls were all watching.

"No more," Ollie told the smiling man. "No more. You have to promise."

He raised his left hand. "I promise," he said. "Unless you call me."

"We won't," Coco said.

He just shrugged, and smiled again.

Ollie put the big key in the gate lock. It turned. She pushed the gate open. The mist outside wavered. "Will the dolls go home?" she said. "All of them?"

"Yes," he said.

"Then this is goodbye."

"Yes." He handed her something. Ollie realized it was her mother's watch. With hands that wanted to tremble, she fastened it on her wrist. He smiled at her, without malice. She wondered suddenly if he hadn't been able to open the gate either. If he might even have *wanted* to open the gate, but couldn't. Because the second key was in the funhouse, and you couldn't get through the funhouse alone. He was always alone.

It was a strange thought. Ollie opened her mouth to ask the question. But the smiling man put a finger to his lips. And then he snapped his fingers. For a second nothing happened. And then, with a crack of lightning and a boom of thunder, the rain finally came. A summer thunderstorm.

And in the deluge, the carnival began to dissolve. As though it were sugar, melting away. Only the smiling man and the gate remained. Everything else—rides, booths, clowns, dolls—dissolved like chalk.

The smiling man gestured elegantly at the gate. They walked through it. None of them looked back, except for Ollie. She turned, right at the mouth of the gate. He winked at her.

And then Ollie found herself walking through the front door of the Egg. Ollie froze for a split second, realizing where they were. And then she was running and hollering, "Dad! Dad!"

"Ollie-pop!" came his voice from the kitchen.

There were people sitting around the dinner table, but Ollie hardly saw them. She hurled herself into her dad's arms. "Oof!" he said, staggering backward. "Well, this is a nice surprise. Were you three puddle jumping? I wouldn't mind some puddle jumping myself. We needed some rain. Everyone's just sat down for dinner, though, so go get changed . . . Ollie, are you okay?"

Ollie had butted her head into his shirt like a little kid and started to cry. Her dad patted her head, looking bewildered. "Hey," he said. "Hey, it's okay."

"I know," Ollie said. She swiped her hand over her wet eyes and smiled at him. "Everything's okay now."

"Mom!" yelped Coco, and threw herself at Ms. Zintner, just as Brian chorused, "Mom! Dad!" and hugged both his seated parents at once. They were all sitting at the kitchen table. Ms. Zintner, the Greenblatts, the Battersbys. They all looked a little surprised at the kids' enthusiasm. Except for Phil. He was looking at them and grinning.

"Go upstairs and get out of your wet clothes, you three," her dad was saying. "You can borrow a T-shirt or whatever. We'll eat when you get back down."

None of them wanted to let go of their parents, but they did eventually. The grown-ups were looking more confused than ever. "I'll go up with you," Phil said.

"Don't take too long!" chorused the parents as they all trooped upstairs.

"I love you, Dad," Ollie said as she left the kitchen.

"Love you too." He was looking in bemusement at her. "Sure you're okay?"

"Never been better," Ollie said.

She went upstairs. Brian, Coco, and Phil were waiting for her in her room. Ollie shut the door and Phil burst out, "What happened?"

"Long story," Brian said. "But we got him."

Coco said, "Brian figured out the clowns' weakness."

Brian said, "Coco got the smiling man to give us a clue."

"And you both saved my life," Ollie said.

"We wouldn't have had the chance without Phil," Brian and Coco chorused, and then they pulled Phil into their circle and were hugging each other tightly.

"I don't remember what happened," Phil said. "It was dark. Scary. Then suddenly I was sitting at your dinner table, Ollie. Like it had never happened."

Ollie shook her head slowly. "The smiling man's last joke, I guess."

"So," Coco said. "It's over for good?"

"Think so," said Ollie, and they hugged again.

Finally, they went back downstairs. A few steps from the bottom, Ollie noticed that her dad and Coco's mom were holding hands under the dinner table. Ollie grinned at Coco. "Hey, Coco, think we'll be sisters someday?"

A smile like the sun broke out on Coco's face. "Aren't we already?"

Ollie turned to the boys. "Family."

"Yup," Brian said.

Ollie looked down at her mom's watch. PROUD, it said on its cracked face.

Ollie touched it gently, and then looked up at her dad. Her whole family was there. "Let's eat," she said.

Turn the page to see where Ollie, Coco, and Brian's adventure began . . .

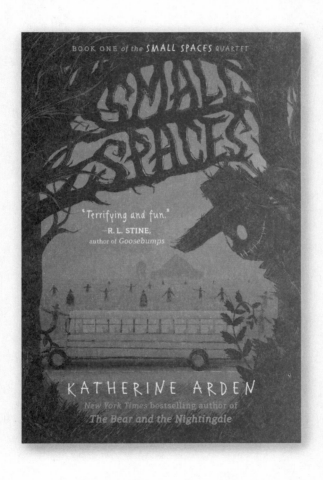

1

OCTOBER IN EAST EVANSBURG, and the last warm sun of the year slanted red through the sugar maples. Olivia Adler sat nearest the big window in Mr. Easton's math class, trying, catlike, to fit her entire body into a patch of light. She wished she were on the other side of the glass. You don't waste October sunshine. Soon the old autumn sun would bed down in cloud blankets, and there would be weeks of gray rain before it finally decided to snow. But Mr. Easton was teaching fractions and had no sympathy for Olivia's fidgets.

"Now," he said from the front of the room. His chalk squeaked on the board. Mike Campbell flinched. Mike Campbell got the shivers from squeaking blackboards and, for some reason, from people licking paper napkins. The sixth grade licked napkins around him as much as possible.

"Can anyone tell me how to convert three-sixteenths to a decimal?" asked Mr. Easton. He scanned the room for a victim. "Coco?"

"Um," said Coco Zintner, hastily shutting a sparkling pink notebook. "Ah," she added wisely, squinting at the board.

Point one eight seven five, thought Olivia idly, but she did not raise her hand to rescue Coco. She made a line of purple ink on her scratch paper, turned it into a flower, then a palm tree. Her attention wandered back to the window. *What if a vampire army came through the gates right now? Or no, it's sunny. Werewolves? Or what if the Brewsters' Halloween skeleton decided to unhook himself from the third-floor window and lurch out the door?*

Ollie liked this idea. She had a mental image of Officer Perkins, who got cats out of trees and filed police reports about pies stolen off windowsills, approaching a wandering skeleton. *I'm sorry, Mr. Bones, you're going to have to put your skin on—*

A large foot landed by her desk. Ollie jumped. Coco had either conquered or been conquered by three-sixteenths, and now Mr. Easton was passing out math quizzes. The whole class groaned.

"Were you paying attention, Ollie?" asked Mr. Easton, putting her paper on her desk.

"Yep," said Ollie, and added, a little at random, "point

one eight seven five." Mr. Bones had failed to appear. Lazy skeleton. He could have gotten them out of their math quiz.

Mr. Easton looked unconvinced but moved on.

Ollie eyed her quiz. *Please convert 9/8 to a decimal. Right.* Ollie didn't use a calculator or scratch paper. The idea of using either had always puzzled her, as though someone had suggested she needed a spyglass to read a book. She scribbled answers as fast as her pencil could write, put her quiz on Mr. Easton's desk, and waited, half out of her seat, for the bell to ring.

Before the ringing had died away, Ollie seized her bag, inserted a crumpled heap of would-be homework, stowed a novel, and bolted for the door.

She had almost made it out when a voice behind her said, "Ollie."

Ollie stopped; Lily Mayhew and Jenna Gehrmann nearly tripped over her. Then the whole class was going around her like she was a rock in a river. Ollie trudged back to Mr. Easton's desk.

Why me, she wondered irritably. Phil Greenblatt had spent the last hour picking his nose and sticking boogers onto the seat in front of him. Lily had hacked her big sister's phone and screenshotted some texts Annabelle sent her boyfriend. The sixth grade had been giggling over them all day. And Mr. Easton wanted to talk to *her*?

Ollie stopped in front of the teacher's desk. "Yes? I turned in my quiz and everything so—"

Mr. Easton had a wide mouth and a large nose that drooped over his upper lip. A neatly trimmed mustache took up the tiny bit of space remaining. Usually he looked like a friendly walrus. Now he looked impatient. "Your quiz is letter-perfect, as you know, Ollie," he said. "No complaints on that score."

Ollie knew that. She waited.

"You should be doing eighth-grade math," Mr. Easton said. "At least."

"No," said Ollie.

Mr. Easton looked sympathetic now, as though he knew why she didn't want to do eighth-grade math. He probably did. Ollie had him for homeroom and life sciences, as well as math.

Ollie did not mind impatient teachers, but she did not like sympathy face. She crossed her arms.

Mr. Easton hastily changed the subject. "Actually, I wanted to talk to you about chess club. We're missing you this fall. The other kids, you know, really appreciated that you took the time to work with them on their opening gambits last year, and there's the interscholastic tournament coming up soon so—"

He went on about chess club. Ollie bit her tongue. She wanted to go outside, she wanted to ride her bike, and she didn't want to rejoin chess club.

When Mr. Easton finally came to a stop, she said, not quite meeting his eyes, "I'll send the club some links about opening gambits. Super helpful. They'll work fine. Um, tell everyone I'm sorry."

He sighed. "Well, it's your decision. But if you were to change your mind, we'd love—"

"Yeah," said Ollie. "I'll think about it." Hastily she added, "Gotta run. Have a good day. Bye." She was out the door before Mr. Easton could object, but she could feel him watching her go.

Past the green lockers, thirty-six on each side, down the hall that always smelled like bleach and old sandwiches. Out the double doors and onto the front lawn. All around was bright sun and cool air shaking golden trees: fall in East Evansburg. Ollie took a glad breath. She was going to ride her bike down along the creek as far and as fast as she could go. Maybe she'd jump in the water. The creek wasn't *that* cold. She would go home at dusk—sunset at 5:58. She had lots of time. Her dad would be mad that she got home late, but he was always worrying about something. Ollie could take care of herself.

Her bike was a Schwinn, plum-colored. She had locked it neatly to the space nearest the gate. No one in Evansburg would steal your bike—*probably*—but Ollie loved hers and sometimes people would prank you by stealing your wheels and hiding them.

She had both hands on her bike lock, tongue sticking out as she wrestled with the combination, when a shriek split the air. "It's *mine!*" a voice yelled. "Give it back! No— you can't touch that. NO!"

Ollie turned.

Most of the sixth grade was milling on the front lawn, watching Coco Zintner hop around like a flea—it was she who'd screamed. Coco would not have been out of place in a troop of flower fairies. Her eyes were large, slanting, and ice-blue. Her strawberry-blond hair was so strawberry that in the sunshine it looked pink. You could imagine Coco crawling out of a daffodil each morning and sipping nectar for breakfast. Ollie was a little jealous. She herself had a headful of messy brown curls and no one would ever mistake her for a flower fairy. *But at least,* Ollie reminded herself, *if Phil Greenblatt steals something from me, I'm big enough to sock him.*

Phil Greenblatt had stolen Coco's sparkly notebook. The one Coco had closed when Mr. Easton called on her. Phil was ignoring Coco's attempts to get it back—he was a foot taller than her. Coco was *tiny.* He held the notebook easily over Coco's head, flipped to the page he wanted, and snickered. Coco shrieked with frustration.

"Hey, Brian," called Phil. "Take a look at this."

Coco burst into tears.

Brian Battersby was the star of the middle school

hockey team even though he was only twelve himself. He was way shorter than Phil, but looked like he fit together better, instead of sprouting limbs like a praying mantis. He was lounging against the brick wall of the school building, watching Phil and Coco with interest.

Ollie started to get mad. No one *liked* Coco much—she had just moved from the city and her squeaky enthusiasm annoyed everyone. But really, make her cry in school?

Brian looked at the notebook Phil held out to him. He shrugged. Ollie thought he looked more embarrassed than anything.

Coco started crying harder.

Brian definitely looked uncomfortable. "Come on, Phil, it might not be me."

Mike Campbell said, elbowing Brian, "No, it's totally you." He eyed the notebook page again. "I guess it could be a dog that looks like you."

"Give it *back!*" yelled Coco through her tears. She snatched again. Phil was waving the notebook right over her head, laughing. The sixth grade was laughing too, and now Ollie could see what they were all looking at. It was a picture—a good picture, Coco could really draw—of Brian and Coco's faces nestled together with a heart around them.

Phil sat behind Coco in math class; he must have seen her drawing. Poor dumb Coco—why would you do that if you were sitting in front of nosy Philip Greenblatt?

"Come on, Brian," Mike was saying. "Don't you want to go out with Hot Cocoa here?"

Coco looked like she wanted to run away except that she really wanted her notebook back and Ollie had pretty much had enough of the whole situation, and so she bent down, got a moderate-sized rock, and let it fly.

Numbers and throwing things, those were the two talents of Olivia Adler. She'd quit the softball team last year too, but her aim was still on.

Her rock caught Brian squarely in the back of the head, dropped him *thump* onto the grass, and turned everyone's attention from Coco Zintner to her.

Ideally, Ollie would have hit Phil, but Phil was facing her and Ollie didn't want to put out an eye. Besides, she didn't have a lot of sympathy for Brian. He knew perfectly well that he was the best at hockey, and half the girls giggled about him, and he wasn't coming to Coco's rescue even though he'd more or less gotten her into this with his dumb friends and his dumb charming smile.

Ollie crossed her arms, thought in her mom's voice, *Well, in for a penny...*, hefted another rock, and said, "Oops. My hand slipped." The entire sixth grade was staring. The kids in front started backing away. A lot of them thought she had cracked since last year. "Um, seriously, guys," she said. "Doesn't *anyone* have anything better to do?"

Coco Zintner took advantage of Phil's distraction to

snatch her notebook back. She gave Ollie a long look, and darted away.

Ollie thought, *I'm going to have detention for a year*, and then Brian got up, spitting out dirt, and said, "That was a pretty good throw."

The noise began. Ms. Mouton, that day's lawn monitor, finally noticed the commotion. "Now," she said, hurrying over. "Now, now." Ms. Mouton was the librarian and she was not the best lawn monitor.

Ollie decided that she wasn't going to say sorry or anything. Let them call her dad, let them shake their heads, let them give her detention tomorrow. At least tomorrow the weather would change and she would not be stuck in school on a nice day, answering questions.

Ollie jumped onto her bike and raced out of the school yard, wheels spitting gravel, before anyone could tell her to stop.

2

SHE PEDALED HARD past the hay bales in the roundabout
on Main Street, turned onto Daisy Lane, and raced past
the clapboard houses, where jack-o'-lanterns grinned on
every front porch. She aimed her bike to knock down a rot-
ting gray rubber hand groping up out of the earth in the
Steiners' yard, turned again at Johnson Hill, and climbed,
panting, up the steep dirt road.

No one came after her. *Well, why would they,* Ollie
thought. She was Off School Property.

Ollie let her bike coast down the other side of Johnson
Hill. It was good to be alone in the warm sunshine. The
river ran silver to her right, chattering over rocks. The fire-
colored trees shook their leaves down around her. It wasn't
hot, exactly—but warm for October. Just cool enough for
jeans, but the sun was warm when you tilted your face to it.

The swimming hole was Ollie's favorite place. Not far

from her house, it had a secret spot on a rock half-hidden by a waterfall. That spot was *Ollie's*, especially on fall days. After mid-September, she was the only one who went there. People didn't go to swimming holes once the weather turned chilly.

Other than her homework, Ollie was carrying *Captain Blood* by Rafael Sabatini, a broken-spined paperback that she'd dug out of her dad's bookshelves. She mostly liked it. Peter Blood outsmarted everyone, which was a feature she liked in heroes, although she wished Peter were a girl, or the villain were a girl, or *someone* in the book besides his boat and his girlfriend (both named Arabella) were a girl. But at least the book had romance and high-seas adventures and other *absolutely not Evansburg* things. Ollie liked that. Reading it meant going to a new place where she wasn't Olivia Adler at all.

Ollie braked her bike. The ground by the road was carpeted with scarlet leaves; sugar maples start losing their leaves before other trees. Ollie kept a running list in her head of sugar maples in Evansburg that didn't belong to anyone. When the sap ran, she and her mom would—

Nope. No, they wouldn't. They could buy maple syrup.

The road that ran beside the swimming hole looked like any other stretch of road. A person just driving by wouldn't know the swimming hole was there. But, if you knew just where to look, you'd see a skinny dirt trail that went from the road to the water. Ollie walked her bike down the trail. The trees seemed to close in around her. Above was a white-railed bridge. Below, the creek paused in its trip down the mountain. It spread out, grew deep and quiet enough for swimming. There was a cliff for jumping and plenty of hiding places for one girl and her book. Ollie hurried. She was eager to go and read by the water and be alone.

The trees ended suddenly, and Ollie was standing on the bank of a cheerful brown swimming hole.

But, to her surprise, someone was already there.

A slender woman, wearing jeans and flannel, stood at the edge of the water.

The woman was sobbing.

Maybe Ollie's foot scuffed a rock, because the woman jumped and whirled around. Ollie gulped. The woman was pretty, with amber-honey hair. But she had circles under her eyes like purple thumbprints. Streaks of mascara had run down her face, like she'd been crying for a while.

"Hello," the woman said, trying to smile. "You surprised me." Her white-knuckled hands gripped a small, dark thing.

"I didn't mean to scare you," Ollie said cautiously.

Why are you crying? she wanted to ask. But it seemed impolite to ask that question of a grown-up, even if her face was streaked with the runoff from her tears.

The woman didn't reply; she darted a glance to the rocky path by the creek, then back to the water. Like she was looking out for something. Or someone.

Ollie felt a chill creep down her spine. She said, "Are you okay?"

"Of course." The woman tried to smile again. Fail. The wind rustled the leaves. Ollie glanced behind her. Nothing.

"I'm fine," said the woman. She turned the dark thing over in her hands. Then she said, in a rush, "I just have to get rid of this. Put it in the water. And then—" The woman broke off.

Then? What then? The woman held the thing out over the water. Ollie saw that it was a small black book, the size of her spread-out hand.

Her reaction was pure reflex. "You can't throw away a book!" Ollie let go of her bike and jumped forward. Part of her wondered, *Why would you come here to throw a book in the creek? You can donate a book.* There were donation boxes all over Evansburg.

"I have to!" snapped the woman, bringing Ollie up short. The woman went on, half to herself, "That's the bargain. Make the arrangements. Then give the book to the water." She gave Ollie a pleading look. "I don't have a choice, you see."

Ollie tried to drag the conversation out of crazy town.

"You can donate a book if you don't want it," she said firmly. "Or—or give it to someone. Don't just throw it in the creek."

"I *have* to," said the woman again.

"Have to drop a book in the creek?"

"Before tomorrow," said the woman. Almost to herself, she whispered, "Tomorrow's the day."

Ollie was nearly within arm's reach now. The woman smelled sour—frightened. Ollie, completely bewildered, decided to ignore the stranger elements of the conversation. Later, she would wish she hadn't. "If you don't want that book, I'll take it," said Ollie. "I like books."

The woman shook her head. "He said water. Upstream. Where Lethe Creek runs out of the mountain. I'm here. I'm *doing* it!" She shrieked the last sentence as though someone besides Ollie were listening. Ollie had to stop herself from looking behind her again.

"Why?" she asked. Little mouse feet crept up her spine.

"Who knows?" the woman whispered. "Just his game, maybe. He enjoys what he does, you know, and that is why he's always smiling—" She smiled too, a joyless pumpkin-head grin.

Ollie nearly yelped. But instead, her hand darted up and she snatched the book. It felt fragile under her fingers, gritty with dust. Surprised at her own daring, Ollie hurriedly backed up.

The woman's face turned red. "Give that back!" A glob of spit hit Ollie in the cheek.

"I don't think so," said Ollie. "You don't want it anyway." She was backing toward her bike, half expecting the woman to fling herself forward.

The woman was staring at Ollie as if really seeing her for the first time. "Why—?" A horrified understanding dawned on her face that Ollie didn't understand. "How old are you?"

Ollie was still backing toward her bike. "Eleven," she answered, by reflex. Almost there . . .

"Eleven?" the woman breathed. "Eleven. Of course, eleven." Ollie couldn't tell if the woman was giggling or crying. Maybe both. "It's his kind of joke—" She broke off, leaned forward to whisper. "Listen to me, Eleven. I'm going to tell you one thing, because I'm not a bad person. I just didn't have a choice. I'll give you some advice, and you give me the book." She had her hand out, fingers crooked like claws.

Ollie, poised on the edge of flight, said, "Tell me what?" The creek rushed and rippled, but the harsh sounds of the woman's breathing were louder than the water.

"Avoid large places at night," the woman said. "Keep to small."

"Small?" Ollie was torn between wanting to run and wanting to understand. "That's it?"

"Small!" shrieked the woman. *"Small spaces! Keep to small spaces or see what happens to you! Just see!"* She burst into wild laughter. The plastic witch sitting on the Brewsters' porch laughed like that. *"Now give me that book!"* Her laughter turned into a whistling sob.

Ollie heaved the Schwinn around and fled with it up the trail. The woman's footsteps scraped behind. "Come back!" she panted. "Come back!"

Ollie was already on the main road, her leg thrown over the bike's saddle. She rode home as fast as she could, bent low over her handlebars, hair streaming in the wind, the book lying in her pocket like a secret.

Ollie, Coco, and Brian's creepy, spine-tingling
adventure continues in . . .

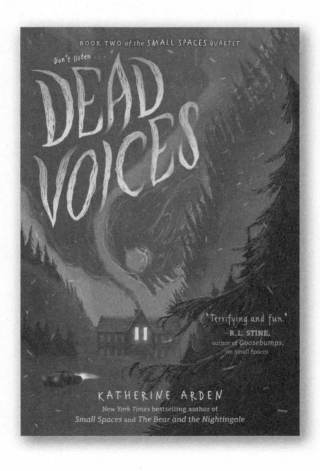

1

WINTER IN EAST EVANSBURG, and just after dusk, five
people in a beat-up old Subaru peeled out of town in a
snowstorm. Snow and road salt flew up from their tires
as they got on the highway heading north. The five were
nearly the only people on the road. *"A major winter storm
is blanketing parts of northern Vermont with eight inches overnight . . ."* said the radio, crackling. *"Be advised that the roads
are dangerous."*

The Subaru kept going. In front were two adults. In
the back were three kids.

Coco Zintner sat in the middle of the back seat,
because she was the smallest. She was short and skinny,
her eyes blue, her hair (Coco's favorite thing about herself)
an odd pinkish blond. Coco peered nervously through the
windshield. The road looked slippery. They were going to
spend the next three hours driving on it.

"Awesome," said the girl to Coco's left. Her name was Olivia Adler. She was Coco's best friend, and she wasn't nervous at all. "Eight inches overnight." She pressed her nose to the car window. She had big dark eyes and the kind of corkscrewing curls that couldn't ever be brushed, because they'd frizz. She stared out at the snowstorm with delight. "We're going to have so much fun tomorrow."

Coco's other best friend, the boy on Coco's right, grinned back at Ollie. The Subaru's storage area was piled high with bags. He reached into the jumble and patted his green ski boots. "It's gonna be *lit*," he said. "Don't look so nervous, Tiny."

That was to Coco. She scowled. Brian gave nearly everyone a nickname. She liked Brian, but she hated her nickname. Probably because she was actually kind of tiny. Brian had the best smile of anyone Coco knew. He'd been born in Jamaica, but his parents had moved to Vermont when he was a baby. He was black, not particularly tall, and the star of the middle school hockey team. He loved books as much as he loved scoring goals, and even though he could sometimes act like a dumb hockey player, Brian was good at noticing what went on around him.

Like the fact that Coco was nervous. She wished he wouldn't tease her about it.

It was the first day of winter break, and the five of them were going skiing: Ollie and Brian and Coco, plus

Ollie's dad (who was driving) and Coco's mom (who was riding shotgun).

Neither adult could really afford a week of skiing. Coco's mother was a journalist, and Ollie's father sold solar panels. But the month before, Ollie's dad had come home from work smiling.

"What?" Ollie had asked. She and Coco were sitting in the kitchen of the Egg, Ollie's rambling old farmhouse. They'd gotten themselves mugs of hot chocolate and were seeing who could build the biggest marshmallow pyramid on top.

Mr. Adler just grinned. "Want to go skiing over the winter holiday?"

"Huh?" said both girls in chorus.

Turned out Ollie's dad had won a prize. For selling a lot of solar panels. A week for him and four others at Mount Hemlock.

"Mount Hemlock?" Ollie had asked, stunned. "But it's not even open yet!"

Mount Hemlock was Vermont's newest ski mountain. It had never been open to the public before. Some school had owned it. But now it had new owners, who were turning the mountain into a winter getaway.

"Yep," said Mr. Adler happily. "They're hosting a few people over the holiday, before the official opening. Want to go? Coco? Do you and your mom want to go?"

Coco had only learned to ski that winter, and still thought that sliding fast down a mountain was cold and scary. She wasn't sure if she wanted to go. But Ollie was already doing a happy dance around the house, and Coco didn't want to disappoint her.

"Sure," she said in a small voice. "Yeah, I'll go."

Now they were actually in the car, actually going, and Coco had butterflies in her stomach, thinking of the storm, the slippery road, the big cold mountain at the end of it. She wished they were still back at Ollie's house, in front of Bernie the woodstove, making marshmallow pyramids. The wind whipped snow across the windshield.

Coco told Brian, in a voice that probably fooled no one, "I'm not nervous about *skiing*." She waved a hand at the windshield. "I'm nervous about driving in a snowstorm."

"Well," said Mr. Adler calmly from the front, "technically, *I'm* driving in a snowstorm." He changed gears on the Subaru. His hair was as dark as Ollie's, though it was straight instead of curly. For the winter, he'd grown out a giant reddish beard. *Keeps me warm*, he would say.

"You're doing amazing, Dad," Ollie said. "You and Susie." Susie was the Subaru. "Dad's driven through a lot of snowstorms," she said to Coco reassuringly. "All fine."

The streetlights disappeared a little outside of Evansburg, and it was dark on the road except for their headlights.

"It's okay, Tiny," said Brian. "We probably won't slide into a ditch."

"Probably?" Coco asked.

"Definitely," said Coco's mom from the passenger seat. She turned back to give Brian a stern look. Brian played innocent. Coco and her mom had the exact same blue eyes, though her mom was tall instead of tiny, and her hair was blond, not pinkish. Coco kept hoping for a growth spurt.

"If we do slide into a ditch," said Ollie, "you get to push us out, Brian."

"Naw," said Brian. "You're bigger than me. You push us out."

Coco interrupted. "You both can push us out. Are there any snacks?"

That distracted all three of them. It was dinnertime, and there were snacks. Mr. Adler was a specialist in snacks. He'd made them each a large peanut-butter-and-jelly sandwich on homemade bread.

After they'd finished their sandwiches, they each ate an apple and shared a big bag of potato chips. Mr. Adler had made the chips too.

"Is it *hard* to make potato chips?" Coco asked disbelievingly, licking salt off her fingers.

"No," said Ollie, in a superior tone. She'd helped make

them. Also, Coco suspected, eaten a lot of them before the drive even started. "But the oil splashes."

"I know what we're making next time we're at your house," said Brian, crunching. "These are *amazing*."

They were scuffling over the last of the potato chips when the Subaru finally turned off the main highway. MOUNTAIN ACCESS ROAD, said a sign. The road tilted steeply up. On one side were trees. On the other side was a gully and a frozen creek. Ollie's dad was driving on through the storm like he didn't have a care in the world, telling bad jokes from the front seat.

"What did the buffalo say to his kid when he dropped him off at school?" he asked.

Ollie sighed. Her dad *loved* bad jokes.

"Bison!" yelped Coco triumphantly, and everyone groaned but also laughed.

"*Motorists are warned to exercise caution, avoid unplowed roads, and, if at all possible, refrain from driving altogether,*" remarked the radio.

"Great," said Mr. Adler, unbothered. "Less people on the road tonight means more snow for us tomorrow!"

"If you say so," said Coco's mom. She gave the smothering storm a cautious look. Coco recognized the look. Coco and her mom were both careful about things. Unlike Ollie and her dad, who were kind of leap-before-you-look.

"Want to hear another joke?" Mr. Adler asked.

"Dad, can't we have a jokes-per-trip limit?" Ollie said.

"Not when I'm driving!" said her dad. "One more. Why did the scarecrow get a promotion?"

A small, awkward silence fell. Ollie, Brian, and Coco looked at each other. They *really* didn't like scarecrows.

"Anyone?" asked Ollie's dad. "Anyone? Come on, I feel like I'm talking to myself here! Because he was *outstanding in his field!* Get it? Out standing in his field?" Ollie's dad laughed, but no one laughed with him. "Geez, tough crowd."

The three in the back said nothing. Ollie's dad didn't know it, but there was a reason they didn't like scarecrows.

That October, they, along with the rest of their sixth-grade class, had disappeared for two days. Only Ollie, Brian, and Coco remembered everything that had happened during those days. They'd never told anyone. They told their families and the police that they'd gotten lost.

They hadn't just gotten lost. But who would believe them if they told the truth?

They'd been kidnapped into another world. A world behind the mist. They'd met living scarecrows who tried to drag them off and turn them into scarecrows too. They'd gone into a haunted house, taken food from a

7

ghost, run a corn maze, and at last met someone called the smiling man.

The smiling man looked ordinary, but he wasn't. The smiling man would grant your heart's desire if you asked him. But he'd demand a price. A terrible price.

Ollie, Brian, and Coco had outwitted the smiling man. They'd survived the world behind the mist and come home. They'd gone into that world as near strangers and come out as best friends. It was December now, and they were together, and on vacation. All was well.

But two months later, they still had nightmares. And they still didn't like scarecrows.

The silence in the car stretched out as the road got even steeper. The radio suddenly fizzed with static and went silent.

They all waited for it to crackle back to life. Nothing. Coco's mom reached out and tapped it, pressed the tuning button, but it didn't help. "That's weird," she said. "Maybe it's the storm."

Coco didn't miss the radio. She was full of peanut butter and getting sleepy. She leaned her head on Ollie's shoulder to doze. Brian was reading *Voyage of the Dawn Treader*. Brian liked sea stories. He and Ollie had both read one called *Captain Blood* and spent a few weeks arguing about the ending. Coco had read the book too, to know what her friends were arguing about, but it was about pirates. She hadn't liked it and felt a little left out of the whole argument. Coco didn't like novels, really. She liked books about real things. Bugs and dinosaurs and the history of space flight.

Brian began to read by the light of his phone. Ollie put her cheek against her window and stared into the wild night. Coco, half asleep on Ollie's shoulder, began recalling the last chess game she'd played. It was on the internet, with someone named @begemot.

Coco loved chess. Her favorite books were histories of famous players and famous matches. One of her favorite things to do was to play online. On the internet, no one could be smug and assume she was easy to beat just because she was small and pink-haired. Sleepily, Coco went back over the opening moves of her last game. She'd played white, which always goes first, and had opened with Queen's Gambit . . .

Up and up they climbed.

Coco fell asleep, still thinking about chess.

Coco dreamed. Not about chess.

In her dream, she was walking down a dark hallway, so long that she couldn't see the end of it. Bars of moonlight fell across the carpet, striping it with shadows. But there weren't any windows. Just the moonlight. It was bitterly cold. On each side were rows of plain white doors, the paint rotten and peeling. Behind one of the doors, Coco heard someone crying.

But behind which door? There seemed to be hundreds. "Where are you?" Coco called.

"I can't find them," whimpered a girl's voice. "I've looked everywhere, but I can't find them. Mother says I can't go home until I find them."

Coco thought she heard footsteps plodding along behind her. Heavy, uneven footsteps. Her skin started to crawl. But she had to find the crying girl. She was sure of it. She had to find her before the footsteps caught up. She ran along faster. "What are you looking for?" she called. "I can help you find it. Where are you?"

Then she lurched to a halt. A skinny girl, about her own height, dressed in a white nightgown, had appeared in the hallway. Her face was in shadow. "Here," the girl said.

For some reason, Coco did not want to see the girl's face. "Hello?" she said, hearing her voice crack.

"I'm looking for my bones," whispered the girl. "Can you help me?"

She moved into the light. Coco flinched. The other girl was gray-faced and skinny. Her eyes were two blank pits. Her lips and nose were black, like she had terrible frostbite. She tried, horribly, to smile. "Hello," she said.

"It's cold here, isn't it? Won't you help me?" She reached out a single hand. Her fingernails were long and black in the moonlight.

Coco, stumbling backward, ran into something solid. A huge hand fell on her shoulder. Coco whirled and looked up into the face of a scarecrow. Its sewn-on mouth was smiling wide. Its hand wasn't a hand at all, just a sharp garden trowel. It had found her at last, Coco thought. It had found her, and now it was going to drag her off. She'd never get home again . . .

Coco opened her mouth to scream, and woke up with a gasp.

She was in the car, in the snowstorm, driving to Mount Hemlock, and her mother was talking to Mr. Adler in the front seat. It was cold in the back seat; her toes in their winter boots were numb. Coco sat still for a second, breathing fast with fright. *Just a dream,* she told herself. She'd had a lot of scarecrow dreams in the last few months. So had Ollie and Brian. *Just a dream.*

"How much farther, Roger?" Coco's mom asked.

"Should be pretty close now," said Mr. Adler.

Coco, a little dazed from her nightmare, stared out the front windshield. It was snowing even harder. The road was a thin yellowish-white strip, piled thick with snow. More snow bowed the trees on either side.

The Subaru was moving slowly. The thick snow groaned under the wheels, and Mr. Adler seemed to be struggling to keep the car going straight on the slippery road. "What a night, huh?" he said.

"Want me to drive?" asked Coco's mom.

This time the usual cheer was gone from Mr. Adler's reply. "It's okay. I know the car better." Lower, he added, "Just pray we don't get stuck."

Now the car was coming down into a gully, the road turning slightly.

But the road wasn't empty. For a stomach-clenching second, Coco thought she was still dreaming. Right in front of them, in the middle of the road, stood a tall figure in a ragged blue ski jacket. It looked like a scarecrow. The figure was perfectly still. One palm was raised and turned out as though to beg. As though to say, *STOP*. The face was hidden by a ski mask.

Coco felt a jolt of terror. But then she realized that the person had real hands. Not garden tools. She wasn't dreaming; this wasn't a scarecrow.

Mr. Adler wasn't slowing down. "Stop!" yelled Coco, yanking herself upright. "Look! *Look!*"

Mr. Adler slammed on the brakes. The car skidded, turning sideways, swinging them toward the thick black ranks of trees. Coco braced, waiting to hear the thump of someone slamming into the side of the car. The person had been *so close* . . .

Nothing.

The car shuddered to a stop, only a couple feet from the nearest tree trunk.

All of them sat stunned for a second.

"I didn't feel us hit anything." Mr. Adler sounded like he was taking deep breaths, trying to be calm. "What did you see, Coco?"

Coco was startled. "You didn't see it? There was a person in the road! We must have hit him!" Her voice sounded squeaky. She hated when her voice sounded squeaky. Had they hurt someone? Had they *killed* . . .

Ollie's dad put on the emergency brake and turned on the car's hazard lights. "Kids, I need you to stay—" he began, but Ollie had already unlocked her door and scrambled out into the snow. It came up to her knees. Brian was right behind her on his side, and Coco, although her hands were shaking, hurried after them.

"Coco!" cried her mom as she and Mr. Adler followed. "Coco, don't look, get back, be careful—"

Coco pretended not to hear. She grabbed her phone, went around the car, and shined the light at the snow. Brian was doing the same. Ollie had pulled a headlamp from the pocket on her car door. The three of them stood shoulder to shoulder, shining their flashlights all around the car. The snow was falling so thickly that they couldn't see anything outside the circle of their lights. Faintly, Coco heard the whisper of wind in the pine needles overhead.

Mr. Adler had a flashlight from the glove compartment. Coco's mom stood next to him, squinting into the snowstorm. Four beams of light shone on the snow. The road was utterly empty. Coco saw the tracks where the car had come down, saw the huge sideways mark of the car's skid. But nothing else.

"I don't see anyone. Any tracks, even," said her mom. "Thank god."

"But I *saw* someone," protested Coco. "In the road. A person. They had their hand out." She raised her own arm, palm out, to demonstrate. "They were wearing a blue ski jacket, but no gloves. Ollie, did you see?"

"I thought I might have seen something," said Ollie. She sounded doubtful. "Like a shadow. But I wasn't sure. There's so much snow. Brian?"

Brian shook his head. "But," he said loyally, "Ollie and I couldn't see out the windshield as well as Coco, since she was in the middle."

Coco's mom gestured at the snow, which was unmarked except for the car's tracks and their own footprints. "I don't think there was anyone here." She started to shiver.

They'd all taken off their heavy coats for driving, and now the snow was piling up on their shoulders.

"I *saw* someone," Coco insisted, but the others, eager to get back into the warm car, weren't listening anymore. She hurried after them. "I definitely saw someone."

"It might have just been a shadow, Tiny," said Brian reasonably. "Or a deer. Or maybe you were just dreaming and you mixed up being asleep and being awake."

"I wasn't imagining things!" cried Coco, wishing *so hard* that her voice wouldn't squeak. "And don't call me Tiny!"

"But there's obviously no one—" Brian began.

"Hey," said Ollie's dad, cutting them off. "Easy now, both of you. Just be glad we didn't hit anyone. Let's get back in the car. It's not safe here."

Coco climbed unhappily back into the car. She felt like everyone was just a little bit mad at her for yelling *stop* so that Mr. Adler had to slam on his brakes and send them skidding dangerously across the road. She was *sure* she'd seen someone.

But she *had* been half asleep. Maybe she did dream it.

As they drove away, Coco turned around and looked out the back window.

Just for a second, she thought she saw a dark figure lit red by the car's rear lights. It stood facing them in the middle of the road. One bare hand was still upraised.

Like a plea.

Like a warning.

"Guys," she whispered. "It's there. It's *right back there.*"

Ollie and Brian turned around.

There was a small silence.

"I don't see anything," said Ollie.

Coco looked again.

The figure was gone.

Coco shivered. She opened her mouth to say something else. But before she could, the car was grumbling up the mountain once more and they had left the gully behind them.

A minute later, two yellow lights shone through the trees. Maybe it was just because Coco was shaken up, but she thought that the lights looked sinister. Like eyes peeping. Waiting for them. She wanted to tell Mr. Adler to turn the car around.

Don't be silly, she told herself.

"Look!" said Brian, pointing. "What's that?"

"Must be the lodge," said Mr. Adler. He sounded relieved. "We're almost there."

They drove under a new, hand-carved sign lit by two old-fashioned gas lamps.

Eyes? Right, Coco thought. *Just lamps.*

MOUNT HEMLOCK RESORT, said the sign. A MOUNTAIN OF AWESOME WHERE WINTER NEVER ENDS.

"That's some weird grammar," commented Ollie.

No one said anything else. The resort drive was the narrowest road they'd driven on, and the most thickly piled with snow. The Subaru's motor whined horribly as Ollie's dad pushed down the accelerator. The driveway turned, and the car skidded slowly sideways, almost going into a spin. The wheels couldn't bite.

"Dad—" Ollie began.

"Not now!" snapped her father in a tone Coco had never heard from Mr. Adler. He changed gears, managed to keep the car from skidding, and then they burst out from the driveway into a snow-covered parking lot. Everyone breathed a huge sigh of relief.

After the long, cold drive, the sight of Hemlock Lodge was like Christmas morning. Warm golden light blazed out of the windows. Well, some of the windows.

"We made it," said Brian happily.

They could barely see the building in the snowy darkness, but Coco thought it was big. It had a—presence. It loomed over them.

"Shouldn't there be more lights?" asked Ollie.

"Power must be out," said Coco's mom. She tugged the end of her blond braid, considering. "They're running on generators. Can't light everything."

"I can hear the generators," said Brian.

Mr. Adler drove across the parking lot and parked

under an awning. Coco could hear the generators too: a slow, roaring noise, like the building was breathing.

"Well," said Mr. Adler, "parking lot's empty. Looks like we were the only ones to make the drive."

"There might be others stuck on the road somewhere," said Coco's mom. "Hopefully they get to shelter. Another hour, and we'd have gotten stuck ourselves. Next time let's listen to what the radio has to say about snowstorms, hm?"

"Deal," said Ollie's dad, and he sounded like he really meant it. "Come on!" he added to all of them. "We made it, all present and accounted for. Grab a bag. The sooner we get out, the sooner we get to bed."

Ollie and Brian fumbled for the door handles and stumbled into the freezing night. All of them padded sleepily into Hemlock Lodge.

Coco stopped dead right in the entrance, staring. Ollie plowed into Coco and had to catch her so they both didn't fall. "Coco, what—" she began, and then she saw what Coco had. "No way."

"Holy cow," muttered Brian. "Where are we?"

The only light in the lobby was from a big, roaring fire. Shadows leaped and swung across the walls; you couldn't even see the ceiling. But the walls were completely covered with heads. Dead animal heads. Coco spotted a moose head with Christmas lights wound through its antlers. A deer head—a lot of deer heads—hung in a cluster. There was a trio of raccoons in a small canoe with paddles. A stuffed fawn in a glass box. Four coyotes looked like they were howling at a fake moon. A black bear stood on its hind legs, its paw upraised.

In the flickering firelight, they seemed to move; their glass eyes shone like they were alive. The bear had sharp white teeth.

"Nice decorations," said Brian uneasily. "Great spot your dad found." There was a giant bearskin rug on the floor. Its claws were shiny in the firelight.

Ollie stepped around Coco and marched into the lobby. "It's great," she said pointedly. Ollie always defended her dad. Coco would have too, if she'd had a dad as cool as Ollie's. Coco had never met her dad. He'd left before Coco was born.

Ollie waved at the heads. "Some people like this kind of thing. And we're not here to hang out in the lobby, we're here to ski."

Brian brightened. "Yes, we are," he said. His green ski boots were draped over his backpack; he reached behind and patted them again. Brian loved all gear, for all sports. Especially his own gear. He and Ollie would go on endlessly about tuning skis and sharpening ice skates. Sometimes

Coco wished that she liked the things her friends liked. Pirate books and winter stuff. She'd have more to say when they were talking.

Two people, a man and a woman, had been standing by the front desk, waiting for them. Now they hurried forward, clattering across the lodge. They were smiling, freckled, happy. Coco was really glad to see them. They made the lobby seem a lot more normal.

"Oh, you made it, I'm so glad!" said the woman. She was thin as a greyhound, sandy-haired, with *cheery welcome* written all over her face like she'd painted it there. "You must be Roger Adler," she said to Ollie's dad. "I'm Sue Wilson. You're the first guests to arrive—a lot of them probably didn't set out at all! *What* a storm! Sorry about the dark." She waved a hand at the lobby. "We thought the fire would be enough. Electricity's out, and we're trying to save on propane in case we're snowed in for a couple of days. Plenty of firewood, though!" She turned to the kids. "You can call me Sue." She smiled at Coco. "You tired, hon?"

Coco was used to adults calling her *hon, sweetie*, and *darling*. Adults who didn't know her mostly seemed to think she was about eight years old. It was the pinkish hair. She *really* wished she'd get that growth spurt.

"Yes," she said politely, gritting her teeth. "I am. What happened to the electricity?"

"The storm," said the man, coming forward. "Wind blew trees over the power lines somewhere or other." He had a beard as big as Mr. Adler's and wore a Christmas sweater. A little belly hung over his belt. "I'm Sam Wilson," he said. "Me 'n' Sue own the place. Pleased to meet you. I guess you saw my little critters." He waved a hand at the wall. "Bagged 'em all myself! Lemme take those." He swept up all three of their duffels before they could respond. "Now," he said. "Enough chitchat. You must be tired. Stairs are this way. Sorry the elevator's not working. Power's out and all. Come on. Welcome to Hemlock Lodge."

Coco followed him gratefully, glad to get to bed and away from the animal heads.

"Big storm out there, Sue," Coco heard Mr. Adler saying. "Should make for some good skiing tomorrow, but it was a tough drive." He raised his voice. "Good night, kids! Be good."

The adults kept on talking, but Coco couldn't hear what they were saying. She padded up the stairs with the others.

They stopped on the second floor. The stairs opened onto a long dim hall. The only light was from a few wide-spaced wall lamps. They cast pools of feeble yellow light. *Must be part of saving on propane,* Coco decided, *keeping it so dark.* She tripped over the last step and lurched into Ollie, who was weighed down by her own backpack and nearly went over.

"Coco!" whispered Ollie. She didn't usually get mad when Coco was clumsy, but they were all really tired.

"Sorry," Coco whispered back. "It's hard to see."

They began the long trudge down the hall. Coco watched her feet carefully, trying not to trip again. "I've got you girls in the bunk room," Sam called over his shoulder. "You"—Brian was it—"are right across the hall. Far end of the hallway. Follow me."

The hall seemed to go on forever. It was chilly. Coco hoped their room was warmer.

Sam stopped at a door that said BUNK ROOM in big brass letters.

Behind her, Coco heard more footsteps coming up the stairs, shuffling along behind them. Must be her mom and Mr. Adler, going to their rooms. Coco looked back. "Good night, Mo—" she started to say.

But her mom wasn't there. The hall was empty.

No—what was that? Near them was a pool of greenish light, thrown from one of the dim emergency bulbs. Cast across the light was a person's shadow. A big broad-shouldered shadow.

One shadow-hand was stretched out toward them.

Like a plea.

Like a warning.

A chill ran down her spine. "Mom?" Coco called just as their door swung open; Sam flicked on a battery-powered lamp. Light flooded the hall, and the shadow vanished. There was *definitely* no one there.

Coco thought then of the strange figure in the road and, for some reason, of the long hallway in her dream.

Her heart beating uncomfortably fast, Coco followed Ollie into the bunk room.

For more scares and thrills,
keep reading for a preview of . . .

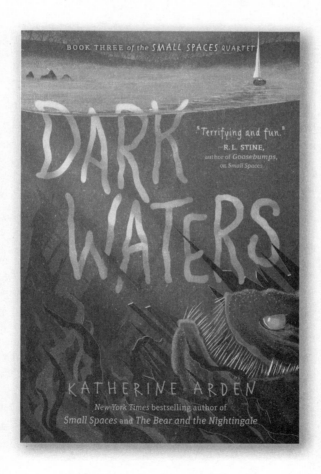

1

SPRING IN EAST EVANSBURG, and the rain poured down like someone had turned on a hose in the sky. High in the Green Mountains, the rain turned snow into slush and turned earth into mud. It washed ruts into roads and set creeks to roaring. It sluiced down the roof of a small inn perched on a hillside above town.

The rain had begun at dawn, but now it was that long blue springtime twilight, getting close to dark, and the inn looked cozy in the soft light. The walls of the inn were white wooden clapboards, neatly painted. The roof was red metal. The sign said MOOSE LODGE, and it swung, creaking, in the spring wind.

The inn's parking lot was empty. Everything was quiet.

Brian Battersby lived in the inn with his parents. The inn had started off as a day spa, inherited from his great-uncle. But slowly, Brian's parents had turned it into a proper inn, with ten rooms. It was a Tuesday in late April, and the lodge was empty. The skiers had all left for the year. The bikers and hikers hadn't come yet. There was no one in the lodge at all except for Brian and his two friends. His parents had gone down into East Evansburg.

"We'll be back in a few hours, with dinner," they had told him. "Don't burn the place down."

"Sure," Brian had said. "No problem." But he'd gulped a little as he watched his parents drive away. He and his friends hadn't been alone in months. They'd been careful not to be alone.

They felt safer when they weren't alone.

Brian and his friends were in the main room of Moose Lodge. It was extremely cozy. There were paperbacks on shelves, magazines on tables, and a huge stone fireplace with a fire crackling.

The door was locked. They felt safe. Well. Sort of safe. They hadn't felt completely safe in months.

"Spring rain is way worse than fall rain," said Brian, shoving aside his disquiet. He'd been sitting cross-legged on the sofa opposite the fireplace, but now he dumped his book to go stand by the front window. He peered past the curtain at the big sweep of parking lot and the muddy, washed-out track of the dirt road beyond. Everything was veiled in rain, water falling like ropes and raising a mist where it smashed into the ground. He added, "Because in fall you're not even *hoping* for it to get warm and sunny. But in spring . . ." He squinted out into the twilight. Was that something moving? No, just a trick of the light.

"You're tired of winter," finished his friend Olivia Adler from another sofa, where she lounged on pillows, wrapped in a wool blanket, a book in her lap. Ollie was taller than Brian. She had big dark eyes and corkscrewing curls that stood out all over her head. She took a sip from a mug of hot chocolate, trying to nab a marshmallow with her teeth. He heard her swallow before she asked uneasily, "See anything out there?"

Brian kept watching the streaming window. "No," he said.

"I don't mind the rain," chimed in Coco Zintner. Coco always looked on the bright side. She was sitting on the floor nearest the fireplace. She was practically *in* the fireplace. She was the smallest person in the sixth grade, and she got cold easily. A stack of books teetered at her side, and she sipped at her own mug, a knitted blanket around her shoulders. Her hair, which was pinkish, was braided down her back. "It's cozy in here."

"Yeah," said Brian, a little doubtfully. They'd spent a lot of that winter holed up in cozy places. Long afternoons in the Egg, Ollie's old farmhouse. Weekend mornings in the small, neat house Coco shared with her mom in downtown East Evansburg. And plenty of time in Moose Lodge, where Brian and his parents lived.

But Brian was tired of being cozy. When you couldn't go out, places stopped being cozy and started being small. He was tired of peering out of windows and into mirrors, looking for anything out of place. Looking for danger.

The main room at Moose Lodge had white walls and old pine floors and piles of pillows on each sofa. The radiator clanked; the walls were covered with pressed flowers and dried leaves and bugs behind glass. Snug, woolly blankets draped the furniture and them. It smelled like orange oil and pine.

The only not-quite-right thing was the blanket that Ollie had used to drape the mirror opposite the fireplace. The second Brian's parents had left, she'd covered up the mirror and wrapped it in bungee cords, all without saying a word.

Mirrors, all three of them knew, could be dangerous. None of them trusted mirrors, especially not Ollie.

While she covered the mirrors, Brian had bolted the doors.

They were fine, Brian told himself. They were *safe*. Turning away from the wet window, he tripped on a pile of books.

"Ouch!" Brian hopped, clutching his stubbed toe.

"Book monster strikes again!" cackled Ollie just as Coco said, "Are you okay, Brian?" Their voices echoed in the empty lodge.

"Yes," he said, dropping with a grimace back onto the sofa. "No thanks to this stuff." He glared around at the books. Twenty or so books, divided into three heaps, one for each of them. Brian pulled the top book off his stack and scowled at it. The title was *Hauntings and Horrors in the Green Mountain State*.

"I think I read this one already," he said. "They're all blurring together."

Ollie's book was called *Giggles in the Dark: True Stories of Truly Awful Hauntings*. "I know what you mean," she said. She pulled a blanket tighter around her shoulders. "Anyway, I dunno if any of it is helpful. Like—listen to this." She read aloud:

> Long ago, the Green Axe Man lived alone on South Hero Island. He used to steal other people's milk, but his neighbors were so afraid of him that no one ever said a word about it. Once, by accident, he cut his hand off with his own axe, but he was

so tough that he didn't care. He just stuck the axe where his hand should be. Ever after, he had an axe instead of a hand, and whenever he went out, you could hear the chopping from far away as he swung his arm back and forth . . .

"Weird," commented Brian.

"Not what we're looking for, though," said Coco.

Actually, Brian thought, none of them *knew* exactly what they were looking for. All they knew was that they were desperate to find it, and they really hoped they'd *know* when they found it.

Coco's book was called *True Tales to Make You Scream.* Slowly, she said, "Maybe no book has what we're looking for. I mean—we've been doing all this research since December, and we haven't found anything. Not even a *clue.*"

"There's something," said Brian fiercely. "Somewhere. We just have to keep looking."

He picked up *Hauntings and Horrors in the Green Mountain State* and flipped a page. Both girls fell silent. The rain wrapped them in its roar, like another blanket. If something tried to creep up on them, there was no chance they'd hear it through the sound of the rain.

Don't think about that, Brian ordered himself.

Brian's eye snagged on a new paragraph.

CAPTAIN SHEEHAN AND THE WRECK OF THE GOBLIN, said the heading.

The wreck of the *Goblin* wasn't what they were looking for either, but Brian paused anyway. He loved stories about boats.

In 1807, went the text, *the* Goblin *was a merchant vessel on Lake Champlain. Her master was called William Sheehan, and folk said that he was the smartest, the handsomest, and the most ruthless ship's captain between Burlington and Ticonderoga.*

But the Embargo Act of 1807 stopped his trade, and so Captain Sheehan turned to smuggling. He smuggled timber to the British fleet in Halifax and smuggled linen back. And he was good at that too.

Until the night he, his ship, and his crew disappeared.

On a foggy night in the fall of 1808, the Goblin *waited at the mouth of Otter Creek to pick up a cargo. But the revenue cutter* Fly *had been warned about the notorious* Goblin. *She was waiting. Sheehan and his men were forced to flee.*

The ships raced across the lake, into the night. The Goblin *led, with the* Fly *sailing after. All night the two ships sailed. Sheehan tried every trick he knew to lose the* Fly, *but the revenue cutter hung on.*

Finally, the fog dispersed and the moon rose, revealing a terrible sight.

The Goblin *was no longer under sail. She was sinking.*
Bow to the sky and stern in the lake. She must have run
aground, but on what? The two ships were in open water.

The Fly went closer. And closer. But before she could
reach the Goblin, the smuggler went down with a gurgle. The
sailors on the Fly waited to hear the shouts of survivors.

But there was only silence.

When dawn came, the Fly swept the area where they'd
seen the Goblin go down.

But there was nothing. Not so much as a floating plank
to show where the Goblin had been at all. Men and ship had
been swallowed by the lake.

But on foggy nights, it's said, you can still see the Goblin
racing across the lake. And you can still hear Sheehan cursing
the Fly for sending his ship to her doom—

The lights flickered.

Brian's head jerked up from the book. Ollie and
Coco looked around too, warily. The lights flickered
again.

"Must be the storm—" Coco began.

And then the lights went out.

Right at that same moment, someone knocked—
boom, boom, boom—on the door.

The three of them froze. They knew better than
to scream. They stared at the door. The only light came

from the fire. It threw their shadows big and strange on the walls.

Boom. This time the knock shot them to their feet and close together. Coco tripped over her pile of books; Ollie caught her, and they stood in the middle of the room, hands gripping tight.

"I didn't see anyone outside!" Brian breathed. "I didn't see a car . . ."

"There wasn't a car," whispered Ollie. "We'd have seen the lights."

"Maybe it drove up with the lights off?" whispered Coco.

Ollie glanced down at her wrist. She was wearing a watch. But it wasn't an ordinary watch. It had belonged to her mother, who was dead. Its screen was cracked; it didn't tell time. But sometimes it gave Ollie advice.

Like now.

It was glowing faintly blue, and a single word jumped on the screen in faint, flickering letters.

HUSH, it said.

All three of them went still. Brian felt sweat start on his forehead. His heart was thumping away, like a pheasant in spring. Why were heartbeats so loud? He tried not to breathe. He could feel the girls' hands sweating in his. Run away? Stay still?

HUSH.

The knocking had stopped. Now he heard the soft sound of footsteps. Circling the house. Going toward the big front window. *Scratch. Scritch.* Someone was scraping at the pane of glass. Brian's heartbeat seemed to rattle his rib cage. None of them moved.

The footsteps went back toward the door. Now they saw the door handle quiver. Very slowly, the handle turned downward. Down and down it went. Brian couldn't see the dead bolt in the dimness. He'd locked it, hadn't he? Hadn't he?

He could hear Coco breathing quick and shallow beside him.

The door handle was down at its very lowest point.

"Run," whispered Ollie, her hand clutching his.

But before any of them could move, a brilliant light cut through the curtains, like a car—a car coming across the parking lot. The handle stopped moving. They all stood, holding their breath.

The lights flickered. Came back on.

The door was still shut. There was no one there but them.

"I locked the door," Brian whispered. "I did. I *swear.*"

"I believe you," said Ollie. She glanced down at her watch again. Brian looked over her shoulder. So did Coco.

The watch was blank now. Just an old digital wristwatch, too big for Ollie's wrist, with a spiderwebbing crack on the screen. They were all trembling.

The headlights in the parking lot cut out. Next moment, Brian heard his parents' voices, arguing cheerfully, as his mom and dad got out of the car. He breathed again. They might have imagined the whole thing.

But he was pretty sure they hadn't.

"What was that?" whispered Coco.

"I—don't know," said Ollie.

"Saved by your parents, Brian," said Coco. "I guess that *is* your parents?"

"Yes," said Brian. They were still clutching hands.

"You don't think anything's still out there?" said Ollie. "Anything dangerous?"

"The lights came back on," Brian pointed out shakily.

Neither girl replied. He heard his mother's footsteps on the front walk. Heard them pause on the front porch. Then she came clattering in, pausing at the threshold to say something, laughing, to Brian's dad. Just like normal.

Brian's mom seemed surprised to see them all standing in the middle of the great room. "You look like baby raccoons on walkabout," she said, smiling. "I guess you got hungry?"

Brian licked his lips and found his voice. "Yeah, Mom," he said. "Super hungry."

Brian's mom had light brown skin and her eyes were just like Brian's. *Like a pond in summer,* Brian's dad would say. *When the light shines through.*

When the inn was in season, they ate whatever the restaurant was serving. When it wasn't, they ate a lot of takeout. His mom, who ran the restaurant during the season, got tired of cooking. "A break, please. I beg," she'd say, and call the Thai place or the burger spot. Everyone in town knew his mom.

Now Brian smelled something yummy. The next second, his dad came in, holding four flat boxes.

His dad said, "We met Roger and Zelda in town." Roger and Zelda were Ollie's dad and Coco's mom. "They're coming up for dinner. Brian, wash your hands, wash your ears. It's time to make dinner!"

Coco said, "Mr. Battersby—are we not eating pizza?"

Brian's dad looked at the boxes in his hands and jumped, like he was surprised. "Oh," he said. "Where did these come from?"

His dad liked to joke. So did Ollie's dad. They got along amazingly. "Ha," said Brian. "Come on," he added to the girls. "Let's wash up."

As they were heading out, he heard his mom calling. "Brian—Brian," she said. "Did you leave anything on the front porch?"

Brian stopped. Beside him, he felt the girls go still.

Brian turned around. "Um, no," he said. His tongue felt sticky. "Why do you ask?"

"Nothing, really," said his mom. "Just found this on the ground in front of the door. Thought I'd check before I chuck it in the bin." She held it up. It was a round black piece of paper about the size of Brian's palm.

Brian hesitated. Then Ollie said clearly, "That's mine, Ms. Battersby. I dropped it. School project."

"Well, great," said his mom. "Glad I could find it before it got wet."

She held it out. Ollie glanced at her watch, as though for guidance. But her watch didn't do anything, and Ollie marched over and took the black piece of paper from his mother's hand.

"Hm," said his mom, frowning at all three of them. Brian supposed they still looked a little freaked, from the darkness and the scratching footsteps. "Are you okay? Probably hungry, huh? Go get washed up. I'll set the table."

They went into the washroom. The second the door closed, Coco said, "Ollie, what's that?"

Ollie was eyeing the thing in her hand with puzzlement. "A piece of paper. Look, someone charcoaled this side. That's why it's black." She held up a black-smudged hand to demonstrate.

"What about the other side?" said Coco.

Slowly, Ollie turned it over. The back of the paper wasn't charcoaled. There were a few words written instead, in delicate, old-fashioned cursive.

bell, it said. Then, *dog saturn day flower moon.* And then, *Consider yourselves warned.* — S.

One shiver chased another up Brian's spine.

"Who is it from?" whispered Coco. They looked at each other. "Is it—is it him?" Her voice went shrill. When they first met him, the smiling man had called himself Seth, and he had seemed nice. He wasn't, though. Not at all. Coco's finger traced the spidery cursive *S.*

Another knock broke the silence of the bathroom. All three of them stiffened, glancing instinctively at the bathroom mirror. But nothing moved in the mirror but them. The knock had come from the front door. Again? But the lights were on.

Brian felt the hair rise on his arms.

The front door creaked. They all held their breath. And then a chorus of adult voices—"So glad you could make it, come in, come in . . ."

They relaxed a little. "It must be your parents," said Brian. "Dinner party time."

Ollie was still considering the smudged black paper, turning it over in her fingers. "What do you think this means?"

"It's a riddle," said Coco. "And I guess a warning, like it says." People often underestimated Coco. She was very small, and her eyes were pale blue and watery. She cried a lot. She was possibly the bravest person Brian knew. "The smiling man likes games and riddles," she added. Coco would know. She'd played him at chess once, with Brian's life as the prize. "Any guesses?"

They shook their heads. Brian frowned. There was something tickling the back of his brain. Something about bells. Bells and dogs and spots. Black spots? But it slipped away before he could grasp it.

Coco said, "Maybe our parents would know?"

The other two looked at each other. Their parents didn't know anything about the smiling man.

Brian silently ran over a speech in his head. One he'd thought out a million times since that fall. Since the three of them—and their entire sixth grade—had disappeared into a foggy forest.

Hey, Mom and Dad. Remember when our whole class vanished for two days and then reappeared? When no one remembered what happened to us?

15

But me and Ollie and Coco lied. We remember what happened—

"No," Ollie broke in fiercely. "We can't tell them. It's too dangerous. The smiling man messes with adults too. If our parents believe us, if they help us, it might put them in danger, and we are *not*"—here she stopped to glare around at her friends—"putting my dad in danger. Or anyone's parents."

"They'd want to know," Coco pointed out. "If we were in danger. They'd *want* to help."

"If they even believe us," retorted Ollie, "how would it go? 'Hey, Dad, you know that there's this other world lurking behind mist and behind mirrors? A ghost world? Well, there's someone out there who wants to trap us there, behind the mist, forever. Got any advice?'" There was a brittle, fearful edge on her voice. Ollie had lost her mother in a plane crash; Brian was pretty sure that for Ollie the thought of losing her dad too was scarier than any ghost world.

Coco said, "We don't have to tell them where the riddle is *from*. Or tell them why we want advice. We could just say it's a school project. I mean, it wouldn't even be a stretch. They've seen our books about ghosts everywhere . . ." She trailed off. She was still carrying her current book, her place carefully marked. It was

16

only one of the millions they seemed to have read since the winter. In not one of them was there a single clue about how to beat the smiling man.

"Not even then," said Ollie. "What if they help us without knowing and that's enough to put the smiling man onto them? We'd be cowards to tell them. Asking for help, *putting them in danger*, just to make ourselves feel better."

"But I don't want to be brave," said Coco. "I want everything to be all right again. What if we can't fix it by ourselves?"

"Nothing will be all right if they get hurt," returned Ollie hotly. "Do you want lights going out and things scratching at our parents' windows? What if our parents disappear?"

"We *can* fix it by ourselves," broke in Brian. "I know we can. Eventually. We just have to keep looking."

Neither girl said anything.

"We can," he repeated, a little angrily. The last time they fought the smiling man, Brian hadn't helped much. Coco and Ollie had outsmarted the bad guy, but Brian hadn't even been there. He'd been trapped in a lodge that had become a strange, vast hall of doors, none of which led where he expected them to. The endless doors had kept him away from his friends until it was all over. It hadn't been his fault, it had been the smiling man's trick, but still. The memory didn't feel good. Actually, more than a few of his daydreams since then had been of him, Brian, swooping in at the last second and singlehandedly saving Ollie and Coco.

After all, why not? He was smart and brave and strong. His parents were proud of him for a *reason*. He was strong enough to keep his parents safe, and to keep the girls safe too.

"Ollie's right," he said to Coco. "I don't think we should tell anyone."

When he took the paper from Ollie, the black circle left sooty smudges on the tips of his fingers.

"I think we should," said Coco. "It's all a game, remember? He's probably *expecting* us not to tell anyone. We need to do something he won't expect." Coco was shy and Coco was gentle, but in the last six months, she'd gotten a lot better at standing up for herself. "We're not getting anywhere with books. Guys, what just happened? The paper is a warning? A warning about *what*? We don't know what he's planning! We—maybe we can't do this on our own."

Ollie had her mouth open on a reply, but a bellow from the great room interrupted. Ollie's dad, who had an enormous, cheerful voice, was calling, "Hey, you three mice! Are you asleep in there? If you want dinner, now's the time. Pizza's getting cold!"

"Um," said Brian, sidetracked.

"Come on," said Ollie. "I'm starving."

Coco scowled. She had taken the black circle, was holding it between her hands. "I still think we should tell them," she said to Ollie's back.

"I don't," said Ollie, heading decisively for the door.

Coco looked at Brian. "We might not have that much time left," she said. "We need help, Brian."

"Yeah," said Brian. "I do know that. But, Coco, what if—what if telling them just means he nabs them instead of us?"

Coco bit her lip. The two of them exchanged grim looks. They were passing through the great room by then, and Brian turned, half reluctantly, to look at the mirror that Ollie had covered up, the second they were alone.

"I can't think, otherwise," Ollie had told them, shuddering. *"Sometimes, with mirrors, I imagine—I'm almost sure I see—things moving in there. At night. I keep thinking, if I go too close, it'll pull me in."*

How much more of this can we take? Brian wondered.

He followed Coco, clattering, to dinner.

Acknowledgments

WRITING A NOVEL can feel like a solitary job sometimes, but it's not. The work and the love of so many go
into each book. When a series is ending like this one, you
look back with joy and gratitude at all the people who have
helped you through.

Thank you so much to my wonderful agent, Paul
Lucas. Thank you to Eloy Bleifuss and everyone at Janklow
& Nesbit, who do so much for so many authors. Thank
you to Stacey Barney, Caitlin Tutterow, Cindy Howle, and
everyone at Penguin Young Readers for all your immense
work editing, copyediting, and otherwise supporting these
books. They quite literally wouldn't exist without you. To
Matt Saunders for your brilliance and your work on all
four fantastic covers.

To the many, many librarians, booksellers, and educators who have read, read aloud, or recommended the

series. My special gratitude to the educators of Vermont. I have had so many wonderful experiences sharing these books with the students of my home state. Thank you especially to Mr. V, Enzi, and the students of Bristol Elementary. I had so much fun telling stories with you.

Thank you to every Vermont bookseller. You have been so wonderfully supportive. Thank you especially to Katya d'Angelo and Chris Triolo and the staff at Bridgeside Books. Likewise to Tod Gross and the staff at Phoenix Books; you guys are amazing. Also to Becky Dayton at Vermont Book Shop and Samantha Kolber at Bear Pond Books. Thank you so much for everything you do for authors and readers.

To the people who read drafts when I needed input, inspired me when I was down, or just gave me the metaphorical kick and told me to keep going: RJ Adler, Pollaidh Major, Garrett Welson, Allie Brudney, Peter Brett, Cassandra Brett, Naomi Novik, Evidence Ardai, and Joseph Coppa Rizzo.

Thank you to my family. I love you guys.

And finally, thank you to Evan Johnson, my first reader and my best friend. Every book is for you.

I was riding on a bus in the fall of 2017 when a heavy fog rolled in. I wondered, *What if this bus broke down?* and started imagining scary things that could happen if it did.

I never thought a book would come out of that day. Let alone four books. I do love it when life surprises you.

The adventures of Ollie, Brian, Coco, and Phil are over, but I hope that one day you will let me pull you into other autumn woods, different dark hallways, new islands of bones. I hope you will let me whisper more stories in your ear. Out there in the dark.

Katherine Arden
March 2022